Wh... Fi... La...ed

For Sally and Dick and their children and grandchildren

OXFORD
UNIVERSITY PRESS

Great Clarendon Street, Oxford OX2 6DP

Oxford University Press is a department of the University of Oxford.
It furthers the University's objective of excellence in research, scholarship,
and education by publishing worldwide in

Oxford New York
Auckland Bangkok Buenos Aires Cape Town Chennai
Dar es Salaam Delhi Hong Kong Istanbul Karachi Kolkata
Kuala Lumpur Madrid Melbourne Mexico City Mumbai Nairobi
São Paulo Shanghai Singapore Taipei Tokyo Toronto

with an associated company in Berlin

Oxford is a registered trade mark of Oxford University Press
in the UK and in certain other countries

Copyright © Kevin Crossley-Holland 1998

The moral rights of the author have been asserted

Database right Oxford University Press (maker)

These stories first published in *The Young Oxford Book of Folk* Tales 1998
First published in this paperback edition 2002

British Library Cataloguing in Publication Data available

ISBN 0 19 275187 5

1 3 5 7 9 10 8 6 4 2

Printed in Great Britain by
Cox & Wyman Ltd, Reading, Berkshire

Contents

North America

To Tell the Truth

Parcels of fibs! Packets of moonshine! Tales so tall you couldn't see the top of them! The three brothers were incredible storytellers. Wherever they went, people flocked to hear them. First they laughed, then they scoffed and they hooted, and they never believed a single word.

One day, when the storytellers were on the road, they caught up with a young princess who was being carried on a palanquin by four sweating slaves. This princess wore her wealth on her sleeve; in fact, she wore it all over her. From manicured fingernail to fingernail, and from elegant topknot to toe, she gleamed and sparkled and flashed.

'Which is worth more?' asked one brother. 'Her wealth or our words?'

'Let our tales talk,' said the second.

'Let them walk tall and count,' said the third.

So the three storytellers challenged the princess to a tale-contest.

'If we show we disbelieve a single word of your tale,' said the three brothers, 'we will become your slaves. If one of us so much as widens his eyes, or raises his eyebrows, or purses his lips, or even catches his breath, we will work for you for as long as we live. But,

1

princess, if you say or show you disbelieve a single word of ours, then you must become our slave.'

Not that the three storytellers needed a slave. But the man who owns a slave owns everything to do with her: her freedom, her time, her energy, even the clothes she stands up in. And the three brothers could scarcely take their eyes off the young princess's gorgeous and valuable clothes.

'Who will be the judge?' the princess asked the storytellers.

'The first passer-by,' said one brother.

So the princess dismounted from her palanquin, and sat down with the brothers in the shade of a huge banyan tree. The storytellers felt quite sure they would win because the princess was just a princess whereas they, they were whoppers in a world of minnows, and no one ever believed a single word they said.

Before long, an old man came tottering down the dusty road. As soon as he had agreed to be their judge, the first brother stood up and began his story.

'I used to enjoy playing hide-and-seek when I was a boy. Most children do. Once, I remember, I hid from my two brothers near the top of an enormous banyan tree. The tallest tree in the wood. Ten times the size of this one!

'Up! Up! Then I lay along a grey branch, still as a sticking point, quiet as a cucumber, and that's where I stayed for most of the afternoon.

'While I hid, my brothers sought. They shouted my name, they even climbed into my tree, but they couldn't find me. At last the blue hour stole through the wood, so my brothers gave up, they went back home. I sat up, then. As stiff as an upper lip! Even though the crows were squawking, it was very quiet inside the tree.

'That was when I found out it's much more difficult to climb down than climb up. Worse, I could scarcely even see the branches below me. So I couldn't get down but I couldn't stay up. Not the whole night! Think what would have happened if I'd fallen asleep!

'What I did know was, with a rope, I'd be able to slide down. So to tell the truth, I nipped along to our neighbours, the ones who live close to the wood, and borrowed their rope—they were always lending us things and they didn't always get them back—and then I was able to slide down from the tree and run home. Whew!'

The first brother shook his head, and looked at the princess, but the princess had neither widened her eyes nor raised her eyebrows; she just nodded and half-smiled.

So then he sat down and the second brother stood up and began his story.

'Inside my brother's story is a second story. On the afternoon he hid from us at the top of the banyan tree, I criss-crossed the wood until I had covered every step of every track. In the green light I looked. In the stillness I listened. Then I saw something move and I thought it was him. I thought it was my brother. So I followed this something through the quaking bushes; but it was a tiger!

'This tiger snarled and opened its mouth—wide. As wide as I'm tall. So I hopped in. After all, there was no running away. I hopped in and, before the tiger could chew me into meatballs and bone-chips, I crawled headfirst into its stomach. Oh yes I did!

'So inside my brother's story is a second story of a second brother inside a tiger. I stretched and kicked and jumped around; I roared and I barked and yelled. The tiger thought there was a whole zoo inside him and he was afraid—afraid for the first time since he was a cub, and he stared up at the full moon as it turned blue-and-green.

'Then the tiger retched, and I turned head over heels. He retched again, and coughed, and spat me out. He spat me flying through the air. Over the trees! Out of the banyan wood! I landed right in the middle of our village.

'After that, the tiger decided there must be dozens of other villages with people more digestible than ours. So, young as I was, I saved my family and neighbours from danger. To tell the truth, I saved them from being eaten. And do you know what they call me?'

'Tiger!' said the princess. But that was all she said. She had neither pursed her lips nor caught her breath but just sat in the shade of the banyan tree, and nodded and half-smiled.

The three storytellers stared at each other. Was the young princess very clever or very stupid—so stupid she couldn't tell the difference between truth and make-believe?

The third brother pursed his lips, and stood up, and began his story.

'Princess! Less than a day's walk from our village, there is a wide river. Not so long ago, I went there to net some fish, but the fishermen there all said they hadn't caught a tiddler between them—not for a week—and their wives and children and babies were half-starving.

'Now I know how to swim all right. I can swim all day long. So I told the fishermen I'd try to help them. I dived into the water, and turned myself into a fish. Yes, a fish!

'To begin with, I couldn't see much; the water was so murky. I nosed around in the shallows for a while; but then I swam right out into the thrust of the river.

'Lying on the sticky river bed was the most enormous fish. Much, much bigger than a pike! As large as a dolphin! There and then I realized what had happened. This monster was always hungry, painfully hungry. So he skulked in the middle of the river, beyond the reach of the fishermen's nets, and snapped up the fish as they swam by. He swallowed them all, and he swallowed them whole.

'That's why the fishermen had caught no fish. And the moment this horrible creature saw me, he grinned and lunged at me.

'At once I turned myself back into a man. Then I drove my sword through the water and straight into the fish's stomach. I slit it open, and a shoal of fish swam out. At least a thousand! And most of them were so glad to escape their prison they never even noticed the fishermen's nets. Not until they had swum right into them!

'I swam and then I staggered towards the river bank. And many of the fish that had escaped the monster and escaped the nets were so grateful they jumped on to the bank beside me. They wagged their tails! To tell the truth, there were far more fish than I could do with. More than enough for every fisherman there. They pelted me with little coins and then they sang me a song of friendship. So home I came, my head full of scales, my hands full of silver!'

The third brother opened his arms and looked at the young princess, but the princess had neither widened her eyes, nor raised her eyebrows, nor pursed her lips, nor even caught her breath; she just nodded and half-smiled. Then the three brothers stared at each other. Well! At least they knew that they were storytellers whereas the princess was a princess, and that if they couldn't so much as make her shake her head, she certainly wouldn't be able to surprise them.

Then the princess stood tall under the banyan tree, gleaming and sparkling and flashing, and began her story.

'There is not much to say. As you see, I am a princess and a rich young woman. I own treasure, I own land, and I own slaves. The reason I'm on the road is that I am looking for three of my slaves who have run away.

'Each slave, as you know, is worth a very great deal—his clothes, his energy, his time, his freedom. So I have hunted high and low, and I must admit I was on the very point of giving up when I met you three. You three . . . brothers! You three . . . storytellers! So now my search is over, isn't it? You know who you really are: you're my three runaway slaves.'

When they heard this, the three brothers were shocked. What were they to do? If they said they believed the princess, they would be admitting they were her three runaway slaves; but if they said or showed they disbelieved her, they would have to become her slaves anyway.

The three brothers sat under the banyan tree, glum as lumps of dough. They whispered, they argued, they didn't know what to do.

In fact, they dithered so long that the old man they had chosen as their judge pronounced that the tale-contest was at an end and that the winner was the young princess.

'I don't need any more slaves,' said the princess, smiling. 'But why do you three men tell nothing but tall tales? Parcels of fibs! Packets of moonshine! Canards! Claptrap! I will set you free on one condition. Go back to your village and tell people home truths as well. Tell them about themselves. Tell them hope and fear and bravery and love. Tell them their own stories!'

The Magic Brocade

O nce upon a time, long, long ago, there lived in a small village in the southern part of China a mother and her three sons. Since the poor woman was a widow, she had to support her growing family as best she could. Fortunately she was very skilled at weaving fine brocade. This material was a speciality of the Chuang area where they lived and it was made of rich fabric with designs of silver, gold, and silk woven upon it. The widow was quite famous in the surrounding countryside for her brocades, as she had a special talent for making the birds and other animals and the flowers that she wove into her cloth appear lifelike. Some people even said that her flowers and animals and birds were even more beautiful than real ones.

One day the widow had to go into the market place to sell some cloth she had just finished. It took her no time at all to get rid of it, for everyone was anxious to buy her work. When she had completed her business she strolled among the stalls, looking at all the interesting objects for sale. Suddenly her glance was caught by a beautiful picture and she paused. In the painting was a marvellous white house surrounded by vast fields and grand walks which led to glorious gardens bursting with fruit and flowers. Between the stately trees in the background could be glimpsed some smaller buildings, and among the fluttering leaves flew rare brightly plumed birds of all kinds.

Instantly the widow fell in love with the picture and bought it. When she got home she showed it to her three sons, who also thought it was very beautiful.

'Oh,' sighed the widow, 'wouldn't it be wonderful if we lived in such a place!'

The two elder sons shook their heads and laughed.

'My dear mother, that's only an idle dream,' said the eldest.

'Perhaps it might happen in the next world,' agreed the second son, 'but not in this one.'

Only the youngest son comforted her.

'Why don't you weave a copy of the picture into a brocade?' he suggested. With a gentle smile on his face, he added, 'That will be nearly as good as living in it.'

This thought made the mother very happy. Right away she went out and bought all the coloured silk yarns she needed. Then she set up her loom and began to weave the design of the painting into the brocade.

Day and night, month after month, the mother sat at her loom weaving her silks. Though her back ached and her eyes grew strained from the exacting work, still she would not stop. She worked as if possessed. Gradually the two elder sons became annoyed.

One day the eldest one said with irritation, 'Mother, you weave all day but you never sell anything.'

'Yes!' grumbled the second. 'And we have to earn money for the rice you eat by chopping wood. We're tired of all this hard work.'

The youngest son didn't want his mother to be worried. He told his brothers not to complain and promised that he would look after everything. From then on, every morning he went up the mountain by himself and chopped enough wood to take care of the whole family.

Day after day the mother continued her weaving. At night she burned pine branches to make enough light. The branches smoked so much that her eyes became sore and bloodshot. But still she would not stop.

A year passed.

Tears from the mother's eyes began to drop upon the picture. She wove the crystal liquid into a bright clear river and also into a charming little fish pond.

Another year went by.

Now the tears from the mother's eyes turned into blood and dropped like red jewels upon the cloth. Quickly she wove them into a flaming sun and into brilliant red flowers.

Hour after hour, without a moment's stop, the widow went on weaving.

Finally, at the end of the third year, her brocade was done. The mother stepped away from her work and smiled with pride and with great happiness. There it all was: the beautiful house, the breathtaking gardens filled with exotic flowers and fruit, the brilliant birds, and beyond in the vast fields sheep and cattle grazing contentedly upon the grass.

Suddenly a great wind from the west howled through the house. Catching up the rare brocade it sped through the door and disappeared over the hill. Frantically the mother chased after her beautiful treasure, only to see it blown high into the sky, far beyond her reach. It flew straight towards the east and in a twinkling it had completely vanished.

The heartbroken mother, unable to bear such a calamity, fell into a deep faint. Carefully her three sons carried her into the house and laid her upon the bed. Hours later, after sipping some ginger broth, the widow slowly came to herself.

'My son,' she implored her eldest, 'go to the east and find my brocade for me. It means more to me than life.'

The boy nodded and quickly set out on his journey. After travelling eastward for more than a month, he came to a mountain pass where an old white-haired woman sat in front of a stone house. Beside her stood a handsome stone horse which looked as though it longed to eat the red fruit off the pretty tree that grew next to it. As the eldest boy passed by, the old lady stopped him.

'Where are you going, young man?' she asked.

'East,' he said, and told her the story of the brocade.

'Ah!' she said, 'the brocade your mother wove has been carried away by the fairies of the Sun Mountain because it was so beautifully made. They are going to copy it.'

'But, tell me, how can I recover it?' begged the boy.

'That will be very difficult,' said the old woman. 'First, you have to knock out two of your front teeth and put them into the mouth of my stone horse. Then he will be able to move and to eat the red fruit hanging from this tree. When he has eaten ten pieces, then you can mount him. He will take you directly to the Sun Mountain. But first you will have to pass through the Flame Mountain which burns with a continuous fierceness.'

Here the old lady offered a warning. 'You must not utter a word of complaint, for if you do you will instantly be burned to ashes. When you have arrived at the other side, you must then cross an icy sea.' With a grave nod she whispered, 'And if you give the slightest shudder, you will immediately sink to the bottom.'

After hearing all this, the eldest son felt his jaw and thought anxiously of the burning fire and lashing sea waves. He went white as a ghost.

The old woman looked at him and laughed.

'You won't be able to stand it, I can see,' she said. 'Don't go. I'll give you a small iron box full of gold. Take it and live comfortably.'

She fetched the box of gold from the stone house and gave it to the boy. He took it happily and went away. On his way home he began thinking about all the money he now had. 'This gold will enable me to live very well. If I take it home, I will have to share it. Spending it all on myself will be much more fun than spending it on four people.'

He decided right then and there not to go home and turned instead to the path which led to a big city.

At home the poor mother waited two months for her eldest son to return, but he did not come back. Gradually her illness got worse. At length she sent her second son to bring the brocade back.

When the boy reached the mountain pass he came upon the old woman at the stone house, who told him the same things she had told his older brother. As he learned all that he must do in order to obtain the brocade, he became frightened and his face paled. Laughing, the woman offered him a box of gold, just as she had his brother. Greatly relieved, the boy took it and went on his way, deciding also to head for the city instead of returning home.

After waiting and waiting for the second son to return home, the widow became desperately ill. At last she turned blind from weeping. Still neither of her sons ever came back.

The youngest son, beside himself with worry, begged his mother to let him go in search of the brocade.

'*I'll* bring it back to you, mother, I promise.'

Faint with exhaustion and despair, the widow nodded weakly.

Travelling swiftly, the youngest son took only half a month to arrive at the mountain pass. There he met the old woman in front of the stone house. She told him exactly the same things that she had told his two brothers, but added, 'My son, your brothers each went away with a box of gold. You may have one, too.'

With steady firmness the boy refused. 'I shall not let these difficulties stop me,' he declared. 'I am going to bring back the brocade that took my mother three years to weave.'

Instantly he knocked two teeth out of his mouth and put them into the mouth of the handsome stone horse. The stone horse came alive and went to the tall green tree and ate ten pieces of red fruit hanging from its branches. As soon as it had done this, the horse lifted its elegant head, tossed its silver mane, and neighed. Quickly the boy mounted its back, and together they galloped off towards the east.

After three days and nights the young son came to Flame Mountain. On every side fires spat forth wildly. The boy stared for a moment at the terrifying sight, then spurring his horse he dashed courageously up the flaming mountain, enduring the ferocious heat without once uttering a sound.

Once on the other side of the mountain, he came to a vast sea. Great waves frosted with chunks of ice crashed upon him as he made his way painfully across the freezing water. Though cold and aching, he held the horse's mane tightly, persisting in his journey without allowing himself to shudder.

Emerging on the opposite shore, he saw at once the Sun Mountain. Warm light flooded the air and flowers blossomed everywhere. On top of the mountain stood a marvellous palace and from it he could hear sounds of girlish laughter and singing.

Quickly the boy tapped his horse. It reared up and flew with great speed to the door of the palace. The boy got down and entered the front hall. There he found one hundred beautiful fairies, each sitting at a loom and weaving a copy of his mother's brocade.

The fairies were all very surprised to see him. One came forth at last and spoke. 'We shall finish our weaving tonight and you may have your mother's brocade tomorrow. Will it please you to wait here for the night?'

'Yes,' said the son. He sat down, prepared to wait forever if necessary for his mother's treasure. Several fairies graciously attended him, bringing delicious fruit to refresh him. Instantly all his fatigue disappeared.

When dusk fell, the fairies hung from the centre of the ceiling an enormous pearl which shone so brilliantly it lit the entire room. Then, while they went on weaving, the youngest son went to sleep.

One fairy finally finished her brocade, but it was not nearly as well done as the one the widow had made. The sad fairy felt she could not part with the widow's brocade and longed to live in that beautiful human world, so she embroidered a picture of herself on the original work.

When the young son woke up just before daylight, the fairies had all gone, leaving his mother's cloth under the shining pearl. Not waiting for daybreak the boy quickly clasped it to his chest and, mounting his horse, galloped off in the waning moonlight. Bending low upon the stallion's flowing mane and clamping his mouth tightly shut, he passed again through the icy sea and up and down the flaming mountain. Soon he reached the mountain pass where the old woman stood waiting for him in front of her stone house. Smiling warmly, she greeted him.

'Young man, I see you have come back.'

'Yes, old woman.' After he dismounted, the woman took his teeth from the horse and put them back into his mouth. Instantly the horse turned back to stone. Then she went inside the house and returned with a pair of deerskin shoes.

'Take these,' she said, 'they will help you get home.'

When the boy put them on he found he could move as though he had wings. In a moment he was back in his own house. He entered his mother's room and unrolled the brocade. It gleamed so brightly that the widow gasped and opened her eyes, finding her sight entirely restored.

Instantly cured of all illness, she rose from her bed. Together she and her son took the precious work outside to see it in the bright light. As they unrolled it, a strange, fragrant breeze sprang up and blew upon the brocade, drawing it out longer and longer and wider and wider until at last it covered all the land in sight. Suddenly the silken threads trembled and the picture burst into life. Scarlet flowers waved in the soft wind. Animals stirred and grazed upon the tender grasses of the vast fields. Golden birds darted in and out of the handsome trees and about the grand white house that commanded the landscape.

It was all exactly as the mother had woven it, except that now there was a beautiful girl in red standing by the fish pond. It was the fairy who had embroidered herself into the brocade.

The kind widow, thrilled with her good fortune, went out among her poor neighbours and asked them to come to live with her on her new land, and share the abundance of her fields and gardens.

It will not surprise you to learn that the youngest son married the beautiful fairy girl and that they lived together very happily for many, many years.

One day two beggars walked slowly down the road. They were the two elder sons of the widow, and it was clear from their appearance that they had long ago squandered all the gold they had. Astonished to see such a beautiful place, they decided to stop and beg something from the owner. But when they looked across the fields, they suddenly recognized that the people happily picnicking by the pretty stream were none other than their very own mother and brother—and a beautiful lady who must be their brother's wife. Blushing with shame, they quickly picked up their begging sticks and crept silently away.

The Tiger's Whisker

A young woman by the name of Yun Ok came one day to the house of a mountain hermit to seek his help. The hermit was a sage of great renown and a maker of charms and magic potions.

When Yun Ok entered his house, the hermit said, without raising his eyes from the fireplace into which he was looking: 'Why are you here?'

Yun Ok said, 'Oh, Famous Sage, I am in distress! Make me a potion!'

'Yes, yes, make a potion! Everyone needs potions! Can we cure a sick world with a potion?'

'Master,' Yun Ok replied, 'if you do not help me, I am truly lost!'

'Well, what is your story?' the hermit said, resigned at last to listen.

'It is my husband,' Yun Ok said. 'He is very dear to me. For the past three years he has been away fighting in the wars. Now that he has returned, he hardly speaks to me, or to anyone else. If I speak, he doesn't seem to hear. When he talks at all, it is roughly. If I serve him food not to his liking, he pushes it aside and angrily leaves the room. Sometimes when he should be working in the rice field, I see him sitting idly on top of the hill, looking towards the sea.'

15

'Yes, so it is sometimes when young men come back from the wars,' the hermit said. 'Go on.'

'There is no more to tell, Learned One. I want a potion to give my husband so that he will be loving and gentle, as he used to be.'

'Ha, so simple, is it?' the hermit said. 'A potion! Very well; come back in three days and I will tell you what we shall need for such a potion.'

Three days later Yun Ok returned to the home of the mountain sage. 'I have looked into it,' he told her. 'Your potion can be made. But the most essential ingredient is the whisker of a living tiger. Bring me this whisker and I will give you what you need.'

'The whisker of a living tiger!' Yun Ok said. 'How could I possibly get it?'

'If the potion is important enough, you will succeed,' the hermit said. He turned his head away, not wishing to talk any more.

Yun Ok went home. She thought a great deal about how she would get the tiger's whisker. Then one night when her husband was asleep, she crept from her house with a bowl of rice and meat sauce in her hand. She went to the place on the mountainside where the tiger was known to live. Standing far off from the tiger's cave, she held out the bowl of food, calling the tiger to come and eat. The tiger did not come.

The next night Yun Ok went again, this time a little bit closer. Again she offered a bowl of food. Every night Yun Ok went to the mountain, each time a few steps nearer the tiger's cave than the night before. Little by little the tiger became accustomed to seeing her there.

One night Yun Ok approached to within a stone's throw of the tiger's cave. This time the tiger came a few steps towards her and stopped. The two of them stood looking at one another in the moonlight. It happened again the following night, and this time they were so close that Yun Ok could talk to the tiger in a soft, soothing voice. The next night, after looking carefully into Yun Ok's eyes, the tiger ate the food that she held out for him.

After that when Yun Ok came in the night, she found the tiger waiting for her on the trail. When the tiger had eaten, Yun Ok could gently rub his head with her hand. Nearly six months had passed since the night of her first visit.

At last one night, after caressing the animal's head, Yun Ok said, 'Oh, Tiger, generous animal, I must have one of your whiskers. Do not be angry with me!'

And she snipped off one of the whiskers.

The tiger did not become angry, as she had feared he might. Yun Ok went down the trail, not walking but running, with the whisker clutched tightly in her hand.

The next morning she was at the mountain hermit's house just as the sun was rising from the sea. 'Oh, Famous One!' she cried. 'I have it! I have the tiger's whisker! Now you can make me the potion you promised so that my husband will be loving and gentle again!'

The hermit took the whisker and examined it. Satisfied that it had really come from a tiger, he leaned forward and dropped it into the fire that burned in his fireplace.

'Oh, sir!' the young woman called in anguish. 'What have you done with it?'

'Tell me how you obtained it,' the hermit said.

'Why, I went to the mountain each night with a little bowl of food. At first I stood afar, and I came a little closer each time, gaining the tiger's confidence. I spoke gently and soothingly to him, to make him understand I wished him only good. I was patient. Each night I brought him food, knowing that he would not eat. But I did not give up. I came again and again. I never spoke harshly. I never reproached him. And at last one night he took a few steps towards me. A time came when he would meet me on the trail and eat out of the bowl that I held in my hands. I rubbed his head, and he made happy sounds in his throat. Only after that did I take the whisker.'

'Yes, yes,' the hermit said, 'you tamed the tiger and won his confidence and love.'

'But you have thrown the whisker in the fire!' Yun Ok cried. 'It is all for nothing!'

'No, I do not think it is all for nothing,' the hermit said. 'The whisker is no longer needed. Yun Ok, let me ask you, is a man more vicious than a tiger? Is he less responsive to kindness and understanding? If you can win the love and confidence of a wild and bloodthirsty animal by gentleness and patience, surely you can do the same with your husband!'

Hearing this, Yun Ok stood speechless for a moment. Then she went down the trail, turning over in her mind the truth she had learned in the house of the mountain hermit.

Kotura, Lord of the Winds

In a nomad camp there once lived an old man with his three
daughters. The youngest was the kindest and cleverest of the
three.

The old man was very poor. His *choom*, his tent of skins, was
worn and full of holes. There was little warm clothing to wear.
When the frost was very fierce the old man would huddle by the
fire with his three daughters and try to keep warm. At night, before
going to bed, they would put out the fire, and then they would
shiver from the cold until morning.

Once, in the middle of winter, a terrible snow-storm came down
on the tundra. The wind blew for a day, it blew for a second day,
and it blew for a third day, and it seemed as if all the *chooms* would
be blown quite away. The people dared not show their faces outside
and sat in the *chooms*, hungry and cold.

So, too, the old man and his three daughters. They sat in the
choom and listened to the storm raging, and the old man said, 'We'll
never be able to sit out this blizzard. It was sent by Kotura, Lord of
the Winds. He must be angry, he must be waiting for us to send him
a good wife. You, my eldest daughter, must go to Kotura or else our
whole people will perish. You must go and beg him to stop the
blizzard.'

19

'How can I go?' the girl asked. 'I don't know the way.'

'I will give you a little sledge. Place it so that it faces the wind, give it a push and follow it. The wind will untie the strings on your coat, but you must not stop to tie them. The snow will get into your shoes, but you must not stop to shake it out. Never pause till you reach a tall mountain. Climb it, and when you get to the top, then only can you stop to shake out the snow from your shoes and tie the strings on your coat. By and by a little bird will fly up to you and perch on your shoulder. Do not chase it away, be kind to it and fondle it gently. Then get into your sledge and coast down the mountain. The sledge will bring you straight to the door of Kotura's *choom*. Enter the *choom*, but touch nothing, just sit there and wait. When Kotura comes, do all he tells you to do.'

Eldest Daughter donned her furs, placed the sledge her father gave her so that it faced the wind, and with a push sent it gliding along.

She walked after it a little way, and the strings on her coat came undone, the snow got into her shoes and she was very, very cold. She did not do as her father bade her to do, but stopped and began to tie the strings on her coat and to shake the snow out of her shoes. After that she moved on, in the face of the wind. She walked a long time till at last she saw a tall mountain. No sooner had she climbed it than a little bird flew up to her and was about to perch on her shoulder. But Eldest Daughter waved her hands to chase it off, and the bird circled over her for a little while and then flew away. Eldest Daughter got into her sledge and coasted down the mountainside, and the sledge stopped by a large *choom*.

The girl went inside, and looked about her, and the first thing she saw was a large piece of roasted venison. She made up a fire, warmed herself and began to tear pieces of fat off the meat. She would tear off a piece and eat it, and then tear off another and eat it too, and she had eaten her fill when all of a sudden she heard someone coming up to the *choom*. The skin that hung over the entrance was lifted, and a young giant entered. This was Kotura himself.

He looked at Eldest Daughter and said, 'Where do you come from, woman, and what do you want here?'

'My father sent me to you,' answered Eldest Daughter.

'Why did he send you?'

'So that you would take me to wife.'

'I was out hunting and I have brought back some meat. Stand up now and cook it for me,' Kotura said.

Eldest Daughter did as she was told, and when the meat was ready, Kotura told her to take it out of the pot and divide it in two parts.

'You and I will eat one half of the meat,' he said. 'Put the other in a wooden dish and take it to the neighbouring *choom*. Do not go into the *choom* yourself, but wait at the entrance. An old woman will come out to you. Give her the meat and wait till she brings back the empty dish.'

Eldest Daughter took the meat and went outside. The wind was howling, and the snow falling, and it was quite dark. How could one find anything in such a storm! . . . Eldest Daughter walked off a little way, stopped, thought a while and then threw the meat in the snow. After that she came back to Kotura with the empty dish.

Kotura glanced at her and said, 'Have you given the neighbours the meat?'

'Yes, I have,' Eldest Daughter replied.

'Show me the dish; I want to see what they gave you in return for the meat,' he told her.

Eldest Daughter showed him the empty dish, but Kotura said nothing. He ate his share of the meat and went to bed.

In the morning he rose, brought some untanned deerskins into the *choom* and said, 'While I am out hunting, dress these skins and make me a new coat from them, new shoes and new mittens. I will put them on when I come back and see if you are clever with your hands or not.'

And with these words, Kotura went off to hunt in the tundra, and Eldest Daughter set to work. Suddenly the hanging of skin over the entrance lifted, and a grey-haired old woman came in.

'Something has got into my eye, child,' said she. 'See if you can take it out.'

'I have no time to bother with you,' answered Eldest Daughter, 'I am busy working.'

The old woman said nothing but turned away and left the *choom*. Eldest Daughter was left alone. She dressed the skins hastily and began cutting them with a knife, hurrying to get her work done by evening. Indeed, in such a hurry was she that she did not try to make the clothes nicely, but only to get them finished as quickly as possible. She had no needle to sew with, and only one day to do the work in, and it was all she could do to get anything done at all.

In the evening Kotura came back from his hunting.

'Are my new clothes ready?' he asked her.

'They are,' replied Eldest Daughter.

Kotura took the clothes, and he ran his hands over them, and the skins felt rough to his touch, so badly were they dressed. He looked, and he saw that the garments were poorly cut, sewn together carelessly, and much too small for him.

At this he became very angry, and he threw Eldest Daughter out of the *choom*. He threw her far, far out, and she fell into a drift of snow and lay there till she froze to death.

And the howling of the wind became fiercer than ever.

The old man sat in his *choom* and he listened to the wind howling and the storm raging day in and day out, and said, 'Eldest Daughter did not heed my words, she did not do as I bade her. That is why the wind does not stop howling. Kotura is angry. You must go to him, Second Daughter.'

The old man made a little sledge, he told Second Daughter just what he had told Eldest Daughter, and he sent her off to Kotura. And himself he remained in the *choom* with his youngest daughter, and waited for the blizzard to stop.

Second Daughter placed the sledge so that it faced the wind, and giving it a push, went along after it. The strings of her coat came undone as she walked and the snow got into her shoes. She was very cold, and forgetting her father's behest, shook the snow out of her shoes and tied the strings of her coat sooner than he had told her to.

She came to the mountain and climbed it, and seeing the little bird, waved her hands and chased it away. Then she got into her sledge and coasted down the mountainside straight up to Kotura's *choom*. She entered the *choom*, made up a fire, had her fill of venison and sat down to wait for Kotura.

Kotura came back from his hunting, he saw Second Daughter and asked her, 'Why have you come to me?'

'My father sent me to you,' replied Second Daughter.

'Why did he send you?'

'So that you would take me to wife.'

'Why do you sit there then? I am hungry, be quick and cook me some meat.'

When the meat was ready, Kotura ordered Second Daughter to take it out of the pot and cut it in two parts.

'You and I will eat one half of the meat,' Kotura said. 'As for the other, put it in that wooden dish yonder and take it to the neighbouring *choom*. Do not enter the *choom* yourself, but stand near it and wait for your dish to be brought out to you.'

Second Daughter took the meat and went outside. The wind was howling and the snow whirling and it was hard to make out anything. So, not liking to go any further, she threw the meat in the snow, stood there a while and then went back to Kotura.

'Have you given them the meat?' Kotura asked.

'Yes, I have,' Second Daughter replied.

'You have come back very soon. Show me the dish, I want to see what they gave you in return for the meat.'

Second Daughter did as she was told, and Kotura glanced at the empty dish, but said not a word and went to bed. In the morning he brought in some untanned deerskins and told Second Daughter, just as he had her sister, to make him some new clothes by evening.

'Set to work,' he said. 'In the evening I will see how well you can sew.'

With these words Kotura went off to hunt and Second Daughter set to work. She was in a great hurry, for somehow she had to get everything done by evening. Suddenly a grey-haired old woman came into the *choom*.

'A mote has got into my eye, child,' she said. 'Take it out, do. I cannot manage it myself.'

'I am too busy to bother with your old mote!' Second Daughter replied. 'Go away and let me work.'

And the old woman made no reply and went away without another word.

When night fell Kotura came back from his hunting.

'Are my new clothes ready?' he asked.

'Yes, they are,' Second Daughter replied.

'Let me try them on then.'

Kotura put on the clothes, and he saw that they were badly cut and much too small, and the seams ran all askew. Kotura flew into a rage, he threw Second Daughter where he had thrown her sister, and she too froze to death.

And the old man sat in his *choom* with his youngest daughter and waited in vain for the storm to calm down. The wind was fiercer than ever, and it seemed as if the *choom* would be blown away any minute.

'My daughters did not heed my words,' the old man said. 'They have made things worse, they have angered Kotura. You are my last remaining daughter, but still I must send you to Kotura in the hope that he will take you to wife. If I don't, our whole people will perish from hunger. So get ready, daughter, and go.'

And he told her where to go and what to do.

Youngest Daughter came out of the *choom*, she placed the sledge so that it faced the wind and, with a push, sent it gliding along. The wind was howling and roaring, trying to throw Youngest Daughter off her feet, and the snow blinded her eyes so that she could see nothing.

But Youngest Daughter plodded on through the blizzard, never forgetting a word of her father's behest and doing everything just as he had bade her. The strings of her coat came undone, but she did not stop to tie them. The snow got into her shoes, but she did not stop to shake it out. It was very cold, and the wind was very strong, but she did not pause and went on and on.

It was only when she came to the mountain and climbed it that she stopped and began shaking the snow from her shoes and tying the strings of her coat. Then a little bird flew up to her and perched on her shoulder. But Youngest Daughter did not chase the bird away. Instead, she fondled and stroked it tenderly. When the bird flew away Youngest Daughter got into her sledge and coasted down the mountainside straight up to Kotura's *choom*.

She went into the *choom* and waited. Suddenly the skin over the entrance was lifted and the young giant came in. When he saw Youngest Daughter he laughed and said, 'Why have you come to me?'

'My father sent me,' answered Youngest Daughter.

'Why did he send you?'

'To beg you to stop the storm, for if you don't, all our people will perish.'

'Why do you sit there? Why don't you make up a fire and cook some meat?' Kotura said. 'I am hungry, and so must you be too, for I see you have eaten nothing since you came.'

Youngest Daughter cooked the meat quickly, took it out of the pot and gave it to Kotura, and Kotura ate some of it and then told her to take one half of the meat to the neighbouring *choom*.

Youngest Daughter took the dish of meat and went outside. The wind was roaring loudly and the snow whirling and spinning. Where was she to go? Where was the *choom* of the neighbours to be found? She stood there a while, thinking, and then she started out through the storm, not knowing herself where she was going.

Suddenly there appeared before her the very same little bird that had flown up to her on the mountain. Now it began darting about near her face. Youngest Daughter decided to follow the bird's lead. Whichever way the bird flew, there she went.

On and on she walked, and at last, off to one side, a little distance away, she saw what looked like a spark flashing. Youngest Daughter was overjoyed, and she went in that direction, thinking that the *choom* was there. But when she drew near, she found that what she had thought to be a *choom* was a large mound with smoke curling up from it. Youngest Daughter walked round the mound and she prodded it with her foot, and suddenly there was a door before her.

A grey-haired old woman looked out of the door and said, 'Who are you? Why have you come?'

'I have brought you some meat, grandmother,' Youngest Daughter replied. 'Kotura asked me to give it to you.'

'Kotura, you say? Very well, then, let me have it. And you wait here, outside.'

Youngest Daughter stood by the mound and waited. She waited a long time. At last the door opened again, the old woman looked out and handed her the wooden dish. There was something heaped on it, but the girl could not make out what it was. She took the dish and returned with it to Kotura.

'Why were you away so long?' Kotura asked. 'Did you find the *choom*?'

'Yes, I did.'

'Did you give them the meat?'

'Yes.'

'Let me have the dish, I want to see what is in it.'

Kotura looked, and he saw that there were several knives in the dish and steel needles and scrapers and brakes for dressing skins. Kotura laughed aloud and said, 'You have received many fine things that will be very useful to you.'

In the morning Kotura rose and he brought some deerskins into the *choom* and ordered Youngest Daughter to make him a new coat, shoes, and mittens by evening.

'If you make them well,' he said, 'I will take you to wife.'

Kotura went away, and Youngest Daughter set to work. The old

26

woman's present proved very useful. Youngest Daughter had everything she needed to make the clothes with. But how much could one do in a single day? . . . Youngest Daughter spent no time thinking about it, but tried to do as much as she could. She dressed the skins and she scraped them, she cut and she sewed. All of a sudden the skin over the entrance lifted, and a grey-haired old woman came in. Youngest Daughter knew her at once: it was the same old woman to whom she had taken the meat.

'Help me, my child,' the old woman said. 'There's a mote in my eye. Please take it out for me, I cannot do it myself.'

Youngest Daughter did not refuse. She put aside her work and soon had the mote out of the old woman's eye.

'Good,' said the old woman, 'my eye does not hurt any more. Now look in my right ear.'

Youngest Daughter looked in the old woman's ear and started.

'What do you see there?' the old woman asked.

'There is a girl sitting in your ear,' Youngest Daughter replied.

'Why don't you call her? She will help you to make Kotura's clothes for him.'

Youngest Daughter was overjoyed, and she called to the girl. At her call, not one, but four young girls jumped out of the old woman's ear, and all four set to work. They dressed the skins and they scraped them, they cut and they sewed. The garments were soon ready. After that the old woman hid the four girls in her ear again and went away.

In the evening Kotura returned from his hunting.

'Have you done all that I told you to do?' he asked.

'Yes, I have,' Youngest Daughter replied.

'Let me see my new clothes, I will try them on.'

Youngest Daughter gave him the clothes, and Kotura took them and passed his hand over them: the skins were soft and pleasant to the touch. He put on the garments, and they were neither too small nor too large, but fitted him well and were made to last.

Kotura smiled and said, 'I like you, Youngest Daughter, and my mother and four sisters like you too. You work well, and you have courage. You braved a terrible storm in order that your people might not perish. Be my wife, stay with me in my *choom*.'

No sooner were the words out of his mouth than the storm in the tundra was stilled. No longer did the people try to hide from the wind, no longer did they freeze. One and all, they came out of their *choom*s into the light of day!

Why the Fish Laughed

As a fisherwoman passed by the palace hawking her fish, the queen appeared at one of the windows and beckoned her to come near and show her what she had. At that moment a very big fish jumped about in the bottom of the basket.

'Is it a male or a female?' asked the queen. 'I'd like to buy a female fish.'

On hearing this, the fish laughed aloud.

'It's a male,' replied the fisherwoman, and continued on her rounds.

The queen returned to her room in a great rage. When the king came to see her that evening, he could tell that something was wrong. 'What's the matter?' he asked. 'Are you not well?'

'I'm quite well, thank you. But I'm very much annoyed at the strange behaviour of a fish. A woman showed me one today, and when I asked whether it was male or female, the fish laughed most rudely.'

'A fish laugh? Impossible! You must be dreaming.'

'I'm not a fool. I saw it with my own eyes and heard it laugh with my own ears.'

'That's very strange. All right, I'll make the necessary enquiries.'

The next morning, the king told his wazir what his wife had told him and ordered the wazir to investigate the matter and be ready with a satisfactory answer within six months, on pain of death.

The wazir promised to do his best, though he didn't know where to begin. For the next five months he laboured tirelessly to find a reason for the laughter of the fish. He went everywhere and consulted everyone—the wise and the learned, the people skilled in magic and trickery, they were all consulted. Nobody could explain the mystery of the laughing fish. So he returned brokenhearted to his house and began to arrange his affairs, sure now that he was going to die. He was well enough acquainted with the king's ways to know that His Majesty would not go back on his threat. Among other things, he advised his son to travel for a time, until the king's anger had cooled off somewhat.

The young fellow, who was both clever and handsome, started off and went wherever his legs and his kismet would take him. After a few days, he fell in with an old farmer who was on his way back to his village from a journey. The young man found him pleasant and asked if he might go with him. The old farmer agreed, and they walked along together. The day was hot, and the way was long and weary.

'Don't you think it would be much more pleasant if we could carry one another sometimes?' said the young man.

What a fool this man is! thought the old man.

A little later, they passed through a field of grain ready for the sickle and waving in the breeze, looking like a sea of gold.

'Is this eaten or not?' asked the young man.

The old man didn't know what to say, and said, 'I don't know.'

After a little while, the two travellers came to a big village, where the young man handed his companion a pocket knife, and said, 'Take this, friend, and get two horses with it. But please bring it back. It's very precious.'

The old man was half amused and half angry. He pushed away the knife, muttering that his friend was either mad or trying to play the fool. The young man pretended not to notice his reply and remained silent for a long time, till they reached a city a short distance from the old farmer's village. They walked about the bazaar and went to the mosque, but nobody greeted them or invited them to come in and rest.

'What a large cemetery!' exclaimed the young man.

What does the fellow mean, thought the old farmer, calling this city full of people a cemetery?

On leaving the city their way led through a cemetery where some people were praying beside a grave and distributing chapatis to passers-by in the name of their beloved dead. They gave some of the bread to the two travellers also, as much as they could eat.

'What a splendid city this is!' said the young man.

Now the man is surely crazy! thought the old farmer. I wonder what he'll do next. He'll be calling the land water, the water land. He'll be speaking of light when it's dark, and of darkness when it's light. But he kept his thoughts to himself.

Presently they had to wade through a stream. The water was rather deep, so the old farmer took off his shoes and *pajamas* and crossed over. But the young man waded through it with his shoes and *pajamas* on.

'Well, I've never seen such a perfect idiot, in word and deed,' said the old man to himself.

Yet he liked the fellow. He seemed cultivated and aristocratic. He would certainly amuse his wife and daughter. So he invited him home for a visit.

The young man thanked him and then asked, 'But let me ask, if you please, if the beam of your house is strong.'

The old farmer mumbled something and went home to tell his family, laughing to himself. When he was alone with them, he said, 'This young man has come with me a long way, and I've asked him to stay with us. But the fellow is such a fool that I can't make anything of what he says or does. He wants to know if the beam of this house is all right. The man must be mad!'

31

Now, the farmer's daughter was a very sharp and wise girl. She said to him, 'This man, whoever he is, is no fool. He only wishes to know if you can afford to entertain him.'

'Oh, of course,' said the farmer, 'I see. Well, perhaps you can help me to solve some of his other mysteries. While we were walking together, he asked whether we should not carry one another. He thought it would be a pleasanter mode of travel.'

'Certainly,' said the girl. 'He meant that one of you should tell the other a story to pass the time.'

'Oh yes. Then, when we were passing through a wheatfield, he asked me whether it was eaten or not.'

'And didn't you know what he meant, father? He simply wished to know if the owner of the field was in debt or not. If he was in debt, then the produce of the field was as good as eaten. That is, it would all go to his creditors.'

'Yes, yes, of course. Then, on entering a village, he asked me to take his pocket knife and get two horses with it, and bring back the knife to him.'

'Are not two stout sticks as good as two horses for helping one along the road? He only asked you to cut a couple of sticks and be careful not to lose the knife.'

'I see,' said the farmer. 'While we were walking through the city, we did not see anyone we knew, and not a soul gave us a scrap of anything to eat, till we reached the cemetery. There, some people called us and thrust *chapatis* into our hands. So my friend called the city a cemetery and the cemetery a city.'

'Look, father, inhospitable people are worse than the dead, and a city full of them is a dead place. But in the cemetery, which is crowded with the dead, you were greeted by kind people who gave you bread.'

'True, quite true,' said the astonished farmer. 'But then, just now, when we were crossing the stream, he waded across without taking off even his shoes.'

'I admire his wisdom,' said the daughter. 'I've often thought how stupid people were to get into that swiftly flowing stream and walk over those sharp stones with bare feet. The slightest stumble and they would fall and get wet from head to foot. This friend of yours is a very wise man. I would like to see him and talk to him.'

'Very well, I'll go and find him and bring him in.'

'Tell him, father, that our beams are strong enough, and then he will come in. I'll send on ahead a present for the man, to show that we can afford a guest.'

Then she called a servant and sent him to the young man with a present of a dish of porridge, twelve *chapatis*, and a jar of milk with the following message: 'Friend, the moon is full, twelve months make a year, and the sea is overflowing with water.'

On his way, the bearer of this present and message met his little son who, seeing what was in the basket, begged his father to give him some of the food. The foolish man gave him a lot of the porridge, a *chapati*, and some milk. When he saw the young man, he gave him the present and the message.

'Give your mistress my greetings,' he replied. 'And tell her that the moon is new, that I can find only eleven months in the year, and that the sea is by no means full.'

Not understanding the meaning of these words, the servant repeated them word for word to his mistress; and thus his theft was discovered, and he was punished. After a little while, the young man appeared with the old farmer. He was treated royally, as if he were the son of a great man, though the farmer knew nothing of his origins. In the course of the conversation, he told them everything—about the fish's laughter, his father's threatened execution, and his own exile—and asked their advice about what he should do.

'The laughter of the fish,' said the girl, 'which seems to have been the cause of all this trouble, indicates that there is a man in the women's quarters of the palace, and the king doesn't know anything about it.'

'Great! That's great!' exclaimed the wazir's son. 'There's yet time for me to return and to save my father from a shameful and unjust death.'

The following day he rushed back to his own country, taking with him the farmer's daughter. When he arrived, he ran to the palace and told his father what he had heard. The poor wazir, now almost dead from the expectation of death, was carried at once to the king in a palanquin. He repeated to the king what his son had said.

'A man in the queen's quarters! Never!' said the king.

'But it must be so, Your Majesty,' replied the wazir, 'and to prove the truth of what I've just heard, I propose a test. Please call together all the female attendants in your palace and order them to jump over a large pit, specially dug for this purpose. The man will at once betray his sex by the way he jumps.'

The king had the pit dug and ordered all the female servants of the palace to try to jump over it. All of them tried, but only one succeeded. That one was found to be a man!

Thus was the queen satisfied and the faithful old wazir saved.

Soon after that, the wazir's son married the old farmer's daughter. And it was a most happy marriage.

The Tongue-cut Sparrow

It was autumn, and the dawn was breaking. The forest was afire with the red of the maple trees; the cranes glided down to the watery rice-fields to dab for their morning meal; the croaks of the bull-frogs rumbled from the river banks; and Mount Fuji, wreathed in clouds, breathed idly and contentedly on the distant skyline.

It was a season and a morning dear to the old woodcutter's heart, and neither his poverty nor the sharp tongue of his irascible wife disturbed his tranquillity and happiness as slowly, with bent back and grasping a stout staff in his hand, he tramped through the forest to cut the day's fuel.

The birds knew him as a loving and gentle friend and chirruped in time to his walk, or flew from branch to branch along his path, waiting for him to scatter the millet grains which he always carried for them in a small bag tucked in his kimono sash. He had just stopped to throw the millet on the ground, when above the twittering he heard a plaintive cry of 'Chi! chi! chi! Chi! chi! chi!'

It seemed to come from a nearby bush though there was nothing to be seen. The woodcutter, sensing that a bird was in distress, went quickly to where the cry appeared to come from, and parting the bush, saw a small sparrow lying in the grass panting with fright and unable to move. Picking it up gently in both hands, he examined it and found that one of its legs was wounded. He tucked the sparrow into his kimono against the warmth of his breast and returned home at once to attend to the little sick creature.

His wife stormed bitterly at him when she learned the reason for his return and showered ill-natured complaints on him at the prospect of another mouth to feed, even though it was such a small one. The woodcutter, long resigned to her harsh tongue, went about quietly and unconcernedly tending to the sparrow. He laid it on an old cloth in a corner and fed it with warm rice-water and soft grains of millet. Day after day he cared for the little bird and with such unfailing devotion that, when the first snows came, its leg had already mended and its body was well and strong.

While it was ill the sparrow rarely ventured from the cage the woodcutter had fashioned for it, but as it became stronger, it became more venturesome. It took to hopping about the straw mat room and the wooden veranda outside, but ever with a watchful eye on the woodcutter's wife, who loathed it and lost no opportunity for attacking it with her broom and heaping on its head the wrath of the seven gods of thunder.

With the woodcutter it was different. The sparrow adored his gentle rescuer and the old woodcutter in turn loved the sparrow with all the warmth of his tender heart. Each evening it perched on the thatched roof to await his return from the forest. As he emerged from the darkening trees, it would set up an excited welcoming cry of 'Chun, chun, chun!' and fly round his head, sit on his shoulder, and pour its twitterings into his ear.

In the mornings it was a different story. As soon as the sparrow saw the old man preparing to leave, it huddled forlornly in the corner of its cage and sang its plaintive 'Chi! chi! chi! Chi! chi! chi!' The woodcutter, equally sad at parting from his pet, would take the little bird gently in his hands, and stroking the soft feathers, say, 'Well, well, now! Do you think I am leaving you for ever? Content yourself, my friend. I shall be back before the last light leaves the trees.'

One morning the old man went off as usual, having first told his wife to take good care of the sparrow and give it something to eat during the day. The old woman merely grunted, muttered a curse, and proceeded with her preparations for washing out their spring kimonos. She drew water from the well and filled the great wooden pail, and in this she placed the fine cotton kimonos to steep. Then the long bamboo poles had to be wiped clean and slung from branch to branch of the trees. On these the kimonos would be threaded from sleeve to sleeve, so that they would dry quickly in the light breeze that fanned the trees.

Next she put some of her precious store of rice-flour into a deep earthenware bowl and mixed it with a little of the water into a glistening white paste. Today she took especial care to mix it fine and smooth, for she was preparing her own and her husband's best kimonos for the ceremonious advent of spring, and it was her custom to soak them in the rice-paste to give them a fine glossy sheen. Their supply of food was scanty enough, but she always managed to save enough of the flour for this yearly ritual.

Leaving the bowl of paste on the veranda, she squatted down by the wooden tub and began the long task of rubbing and steeping, steeping and rubbing, until the kimonos were clean and fresh as young bamboo shoots.

It was long past midday before she finished, and the poor sparrow, now ravenous, was singing its best to win the old woman's heart and her millet grains. But to no avail. She continued with her washing as if the bird did not exist, and the sour lines on her face told it that she had no intention of giving it anything. Dejected, it flew to the veranda, and seeing the bowl, perched on its rim. Whatever the white paste was inside, it looked good, smelt good, and, 'It tastes delicious, chun! chun!' cried the sparrow as it withdrew its beak and the rich rice-paste passed over its tongue.

'Oh! Oh! Oh! What a dish! What a find!' it chirruped in delight, and down went its beak again and did not reappear until the bottom of the bowl gleamed bare and clear in the midday winter sun. The sparrow hopped from the bowl on to the veranda and was preening itself in the sunshine when the old woman returned with the kimonos to dip them in the paste. When she saw the empty bowl, her whole body began shaking with hatred and anger, and seizing the sparrow before it had time to dodge out of her reach, she yelled, 'You did it! You did it! You gluttonous, grasping scavenger! Now I'll put an end to that pretty song of yours for good. Do you hear? For good! For good!'

As her voice rose to a screech, she pulled a pair of scissors from her pocket and forcing the sparrow's beak apart, slit its tongue with the sharp blades and flung the poor creature to the ground. The sparrow turned and churned the dust and its wings beat the earth in agony. Cries of pain formed in its throat, but no sounds came from its beak. Several times it tried to lift itself from the earth, but its sufferings seemed to anchor it. Round and round it struggled and fluttered. Then, with one last effort of its little pain-filled body, it rose in the air and disappeared over the tree-tops of the forest.

Returning home that evening, the woodcutter was greatly surprised not to hear his usual welcome as he approached the hut. His pet was nowhere to be seen. And no glad 'Chun, chun, chun!' broke the evening stillness. Perturbed and uneasy, he went straight to its cage but found it empty. Turning to his wife he asked, 'Where is our little Chunko?'

'The nasty creature ate every morsel of my rice-paste: so I slit its tongue and drove it away. Wherever it is now, it is better than being here; for I could stand the wretch no longer,' his wife replied in anger.

'Oh, how pitiful! How pitiful!' cried the woodcutter in anguish, as if his own tongue had suffered the fate of his little sparrow. 'What a cruel, what a wicked thing to do! You will suffer for this evil, indeed! Where is my little friend now? Where can it have gone?'

'The further the better for my part,' snapped back his wife, untouched by her husband's distress. 'And a good riddance into the bargain!'

That night the woodcutter could not sleep. He turned and tossed in wakeful anxiety for his little bird, calling out from time to time in the hope that it might answer. When at last light came, he rose and dressed quickly and went to the forest in search of it. For a long time he wandered calling out, 'Tongue-cut sparrow, where are you? Where are you? Come to me, my little Chunko!'

But only the croaks of the bull-frogs, the cries of the cranes high overhead, and the chirrupings of the forest birds answered; the gay, glad song of 'Chun, chun, chun!' was nowhere to be heard. All the morning he searched and far into the afternoon, forgetful of food or weariness and with thought only for his little friend. As the evening light settled over the forest, turning the shadowy trees to the shapes of menacing giants and ferocious beasts, he sat down at the foot of a tree, exhausted and desolate, but still calling out, 'My little tongue-cut Chunko, where are you? Where are you?'

Overcome by the sadness in the woodcutter's voice, some sparrows, perched above him in the tree-tops, flew down to greet and to talk to him. The old man was overjoyed to see them and begged them for news of his friend. The birds were deeply moved by the woodcutter's grief, and twittering among themselves, they finally said, 'Grandpapa San, we know your Chunko well and where it lives. Follow us and we shall lead you to its home.'

The woodcutter, all thought of his weariness gone, sprang up and started out after the sparrows. He followed in the darkness for a long time, till at last they came to a clearing and there, in the midst of a moss-covered patch, surrounded by bamboo saplings, was a house gaily lit with lanterns hanging from the thatched eaves.

Immediately a throng of sparrows came out to welcome him. They lined up before him and bowed deeply until their beaks touched the ground. They showed him into the house with every courtesy, helping him to remove his straw-bound clogs and putting soft slippers on his feet. They led him along a corridor of shining cedar wood to a room of newly-laid straw matting. Here he courteously knocked off the soft slippers and entered in his cloth socks. The sparrows pulled back the decorated sliding screens of an inner room to reveal little Chunko surrounded by a flock of attendants, sitting on the floor awaiting his arrival.

'Oh! little friend, I have found you at last! I have looked in every tree in the forest to bring you back and comfort you and ask your forgiveness for the wickedness of my wife. And your tongue? Is it healed? How I grieved for you! I am overjoyed to see you again,' the woodcutter cried with the tears trickling down his cheeks.

'Thank you, thank you, Grandpapa! I am completely healed. Thank you! I, too, am overjoyed to see you,' wept the little sparrow and flew to the shoulder of the old man, who stroked it gently and tenderly.

'But, now, you must meet my parents,' said Chunko.

So saying, the sparrow led him into another room and presented him to its parents, who knew already of their child's rescue from death and the great kindness bestowed upon it during the long days of its illness by the old woodcutter. Bowing low, the parent birds expressed their grateful thanks to the old man, murmuring with deep gratitude that their obligation to him could never be repaid. They summoned the serving birds and instructed them to prepare a feast.

As an honoured guest, they seated the old man nearest to the alcove in which a silk scroll inscribed with a poem hung. The old woodcutter was lost in wonder at the great beauty of the table and its furnishings. The chopsticks were of pure ivory, the soup-bowls of gilded lacquer, and the serving dishes were from the finest kilns in the land. Exquisite dish followed exquisite dish and all was served with delicacy and taste.

After the feast a group of elegant and gaily-kimonoed young sparrows entered, and to the accompaniment of two older birds—one who plucked the strings of the samisen and the other who chanted the words of the song—they performed the famous classical dance, 'The Wind among the Bamboo Leaves'. At that moment a light wind rose in the bamboo grove outside, shaking the branches and rustling the leaves in harmony with the sweet voices of the dancers as they joined in the words of the song.

As the dance finished and the wind among the leaves died away, the dancers bowed gracefully before disappearing into the inner room. Almost immediately they were followed by a second group, all carrying many-coloured paper parasols. The music of the samisen became sparkling and gay; the parasols twirled and spun; the dancers' feet beat 'tom, tom, tom'; and the lanterns hanging from the eaves swayed in rhythm with the dance. The woodcutter's eyes sparkled, he beat time with his chopsticks, and he was lost to all but the merriment of the wonderful scene.

The music faded and the dancers bowed and pattered out. Thoughts of his wife began to trouble the old man and reluctantly he told his hosts that he must return home. The sparrows were deeply disappointed and tried hard to dissuade him, but the woodcutter said that it would be unkind to leave his wife alone any longer and that he must return. Never before had he known that life could be so good, so gay, and so gracious; never would he forget this evening and the rare kindness of his honourable hosts. But now he must leave. They pressed him no further.

Then the father bird spoke, 'Honourable and gentle woodcutter, we are deeply conscious of your greatness of heart and the loving care you bestowed upon our only child. You came to love Chunko as your own, and Chunko loved you as a father. We want you to remember that our humble home will always be yours, our unworthy food will be your food, and all we possess we shall always share with you. But tonight we wish you to accept a gift from us as a token of our unbounded gratitude.'

At this, two wicker baskets were brought before the old man by the serving birds and placed on the floor.

'Here are two baskets,' continued the father bird. 'One is large and heavy; the other is small and light. Whichever you choose, my honourable friend, is yours, and is given with the heartfelt wishes of us all.'

The woodcutter was deeply moved and tears filled his eyes. He looked at the parent birds for a long time unable to speak. At last he said, 'I have no wish for many possessions in this world. I am old and frail and my time on earth will not be much longer. My needs are very small. So I shall accept most gratefully the smaller basket.'

The serving birds carried the basket to the entrance hall and there they tied it on the old man's back and helped him on with his clogs. All the sparrows gathered at the door to wish him farewell.

'Goodbye, my little friends. Goodbye, little Chunko! Look after yourself! It was a wonderful evening and I shall never forget it,' said the old man and bowed courteously many times. With a final wave of his hand, he left the grove and disappeared into the blackness of the forest with a flock of sparrows flying in front to put him on his way.

When he reached home the clouds were already glowing with the morning sun. He found his wife as angry as a November storm because of his long absence and her fury was unleashed over the poor woodcutter's head. Suddenly catching sight of the basket on his back, her tirade stopped.

'What's that you've got on your back?' she said in a voice filled with curiosity.

'It is a gift from the parents of little Chunko,' replied her husband.

'Well, why do you stupidly stand there and not tell me? What is it? What have the creatures given you? Don't stand there like someone dead! Off with it from your back and see what's inside!' carped her greedy voice, and grasping the straps, she trailed the basket from his shoulders and tore open the lid.

A burst of dazzling brightness momentarily blinded her avaricious eyes, for inside lay kimonos soft as the morning dew and dyed with the petals of wild flowers, rolls of silk spun from the plumes of cranes, branches of coral from the seas of heaven, and ornaments sparkling brighter than the eyes of lovers. They both gazed in silence, dazed and bewildered; these were riches beyond even the world of their imagination. 'A poet's dreamings,' murmured the old man, and fell into silence again. The old woman drove in her hands and let the ornaments trickle through her trembling fingers.

'We are rich! We are rich! We are rich!' she repeated over and over.

Later that day the old man recounted the story of his adventure from the beginning. When his wife heard that he had chosen the small basket when he might have had the larger one, she burst out in anger.

'What sort of a stupid husband have I? You bring home a small basket when with a little more trouble you could have brought home twice the quantity of treasures. We would have been doubly rich. This very day I will go myself and pay the birds a visit. I shall not be so senseless as you. I will see to it that I return with the big basket.'

The old woodcutter argued and pleaded with her to be content with what they had. They were rich beyond the wealth of kings—enough for them and all the generations of their relatives. But her ears were stopped by the thoughts of her clutching, covetous mind, and grasping her outer wrap, she rushed out in a fever of anticipation.

As she had a good idea of the whereabouts of the sparrow's house from her husband's description, she reached the bamboo grove before midday. 'Tongue-cut sparrow, where are you? Where are you, little Chunko? Come to me!' she cried.

But her voice was harsh and even her smooth pleadings could not conceal the cantankerousness of her nature. It was a long time before any bird appeared. At last two sparrows flew from the house and curtly asked her what was her business.

'I have come to see my friend, little Chunko,' she answered.

Without saying another word, the sparrows led her to the

house, where she was met by the serving birds, who, also quiet and reserved, led her along the corridor to the inner room. She was in so much hurry that she refused to stop to remove her wooden clogs and the sparrows were horrified at such insolent bad manners. When little Chunko saw her, it flew terrified to a roof beam.

'Ah! I see that you are quite recovered, my little pet. I knew I had not really hurt you!' she said in a honeyed voice. Then forgetting all womanly modesty and oblivious of the cold atmosphere about her, she blurted out, 'I am in a hurry. Please do not bother to dance for me. And I have no time to eat anything either. But I have come a long way, so please give me a souvenir of my visit quickly, as I must return at once.'

In silence the serving birds brought in two baskets, one large and heavy and one small and light, and placed them before her.

'As a parting gift from us, please accept one of these baskets,' said the father bird. 'As you see, one is large and heavy and the other is small and light. Whichever you choose is yours.'

Barely waiting for the parent bird to finish speaking, the old woman pointed eagerly to the large basket.

'It is yours,' said the bird gravely.

In the hall, with many shoves and heaves, the sparrows hoisted the basket on to the old woman's back and bowed her in silence out of the door. She wasted no time in bows in return but hastened off into the cover of the forest, staggering under the weight of the basket.

No sooner was she out of sight of the bamboo grove than she dragged the basket from her back and flung open the lid. Horrified she fell back as monsters and devils poured out with eyes shooting flames, mouths belching smoke, and ears emitting sulphurous clouds. Some had seven horned heads that lolloped and rolled on their slithery bodies, some had arms that writhed and coiled like snakes waving and searching blindly through the sulphurous air. Bodies, tenuous and billowing and spiked with the horns of great sea-shells, floated upwards and outwards; among them one in the semblance of a young girl with floating black hair whose sole feature was a single eyeball set in the centre of a blank, white face. All these rose and bent and drifted over the horror-stricken body of the old woman.

'Where is this grasping, greedy, wicked woman?' they screamed, and the snaky arms groped and twisted round her. Suddenly all the monsters shrieked with one searing, ear-splitting voice, 'There she is! There is the evil-minded hag! Let us blow sulphur in her eyes and they'll be greedy no longer. Let us embrace her to our shell-spiked breasts and destroy the wickedness in her flesh. Let us peck and nibble her with our forked tongues until she dies, dies, dies.'

Panic-stricken the old woman fled, all feeling frozen out of her body. Through bush and bramble and water she sped with the swiftness of the wind, the monsters in mad pursuit behind.

'Peck her, nibble her, blow sulphur in her eyes; puncture her flesh with our spiked breasts,' they screeched.

'Oh! Buddha! Help me! Save me from these devils!' the old woman screamed.

Their bodies floated over her, their blindly groping arms stretched out to enfold her. Suddenly there was a burst of light among the trees. It was the setting sun showering the sky with rose and gold. As the golden radiance flooded the forest the monsters huddled back with yells of dismay, and turning in panic, they vanished into the darkness of the trees and were seen no more.

The old woman stopped, breathless and trembling, her body sick in every pore. The radiance in the forest was now dying, and dreading the monsters' return, she started off again, exhausted and trembling at every step.

When she reached home, her husband, shocked at her pitiful state, ran out and helped her to the veranda, where she sat panting for some time before she was able to speak.

'What has happened to you? What has happened to you? Do please tell me!' pleaded the old man.

His wife, after telling him her story, said, 'I have been ill-natured, evil-minded, and greedy all my life. This is the retribution I have deserved. I have had my lesson, a bitter one, but not perhaps so bitter as the life I have led you. Now I know how evil I have been. From this hour onwards, I will mend my ways. I will try to be a kinder, gentler woman and a better wife to you, my dear husband.'

He placed his hand on her shoulder and they both knew that the bad days were gone for ever. For the years that were left to them they knew no want and never a harsh word passed the old woman's lips. The sparrows became their closest friends and each paid regular visits to the other's home. Long after the old couple died, the sparrows commemorated the story of the old man and the old woman in a song, and for all I know they sing it to their children still.

The Son of Seven Queens

Once upon a time there lived a king who had seven queens, but no children. This was a great grief to him, especially when he remembered that on his death there would be no heir to inherit the kingdom.

Now it happened one day that a poor old fakir came to the king, and said, 'Your prayers are heard, your desire shall be accomplished, and one of your seven queens shall bear a son.'

The king's delight at this promise knew no bounds, and he gave orders for appropriate festivities to be prepared against the coming event throughout the length and breadth of the land.

Meanwhile the seven queens lived luxuriously in a splendid palace, attended by hundreds of female slaves, and fed to their hearts' content on sweetmeats and confectionery.

Now the king was very fond of hunting, and one day, before he started, the seven queens sent him a message saying, 'May it please our dearest lord not to hunt towards the north today, for we have dreamt bad dreams, and fear lest evil should befall you.'

The king, to allay their anxiety, promised regard for their wishes, and set out towards the south; but as luck would have it, although he hunted diligently, he found no game. Nor had he more success to the east or west, so that, being a keen sportsman, and determined not to go home empty-handed, he forgot all about his promise, and turned to the north.

Here also he was at first unsuccessful, but just as he made up his mind to give up for that day, a white hind with golden horns and silver hoofs flashed past him into a thicket. So quickly did it pass that he scarcely saw it; nevertheless a burning desire to capture and possess the beautiful strange creature filled his breast. He instantly ordered his attendants to form a ring round the thicket, and so encircle the hind; then, gradually narrowing the circle, he pressed forward till he could distinctly see the white hind panting in the midst. Nearer and nearer he advanced, till, just as he thought to lay hold of the beautiful strange creature, it gave one mighty bound, leapt clean over the king's head, and fled towards the mountains.

Forgetful of all else, the king, setting spurs to his horse, followed at full speed. On, on he galloped, leaving his retinue far behind, keeping the white hind in view, never drawing bridle, until, finding himself in a narrow ravine with no outlet, he reined in his steed. Before him stood a miserable hovel, into which, being tired after his long, unsuccessful chase, he entered to ask for a drink of water. An old woman, seated in the hut at a spinning-wheel, answered his request by calling to her daughter, and immediately from an inner room came a maiden so lovely and charming, so white-skinned and golden-haired, that the king was transfixed by astonishment at seeing so beautiful a sight in the wretched hovel.

She held the vessel of water to the king's lips, and as he drank he looked into her eyes, and then it became clear to him that the girl was none other than the white hind with the golden horns and silver feet he had chased so far.

Her beauty bewitched him, so he fell on his knees, begging her to return with him as his bride; but she only laughed, saying seven queens were quite enough even for a king to manage. However, when he would take no refusal, but implored her to have pity on him, promising everything she could desire, she replied, 'Give me the eyes of your seven queens, and then perhaps I may believe you mean what you say.'

The king was so carried away by the glamour of the white hind's magical beauty, that he went home at once, had the eyes of his seven queens taken out, and, after throwing the poor blind creatures into a noisome dungeon whence they could not escape, set off once more for the hovel in the ravine, bearing with him his horrible offering. But the white hind only laughed cruelly when she saw the fourteen eyes, and threading them as a necklace, flung it round her mother's neck saying, 'Wear that, little mother, as a keepsake, whilst I am away in the king's palace.'

Then she went back with the bewitched monarch, as his bride, and he gave her the seven queens' rich clothes and jewels to wear, the seven queens' palace to live in, and the seven queens' slaves to wait upon her; so that she really had everything a witch could desire.

Now, very soon after the seven wretched hapless queens had their eyes torn out, and were cast into prison, a baby was born to the youngest of the queens. It was a handsome boy, but the other queens were very jealous that the youngest amongst them should be so fortunate. But though at first they disliked the handsome little boy, he soon proved so useful to them, that ere long they all looked on him as their son. Almost as soon as he could walk about he began scraping at the mud wall of their dungeon, and in an incredibly short space of time had made a hole big enough for him to crawl through. Through this he disappeared, returning in an hour or so laden with sweetmeats, which he divided equally amongst the seven blind queens.

As he grew older he enlarged the hole, and slipped out two or three times every day to play with the little nobles in the town. No one knew who the tiny boy was, but everybody liked him, and he was so full of funny tricks and antics, so merry and bright, that he was sure to be rewarded by some girdle-cakes, a handful of parched grain, or some sweetmeats. All these things he brought home to his seven mothers, as he loved to call the seven blind queens, who by his help lived on in their dungeon when all the world thought they had starved to death ages before.

At last, when he was quite a big lad, he one day took his bow and arrow, and went out to seek for game. Coming by chance past the palace where the white hind lived in wicked splendour and magnificence, he saw some pigeons fluttering round the white marble turrets, and, taking good aim, shot one dead. It came tumbling past the very window where the white queen was sitting; she rose to see what was the matter, and looked out. At the first glance of the handsome young lad standing there bow in hand, she knew by witchcraft that it was the king's son.

She nearly died of envy and spite, determining to destroy the lad without delay; therefore, sending a servant to bring him to her presence, she asked him if he would sell her the pigeon he had just shot.

'No,' replied the sturdy lad, 'the pigeon is for my seven blind mothers, who live in the noisome dungeon, and who would die if I did not bring them food.'

'Poor souls!' cried the cunning white witch. 'Would you not like to bring them their eyes again? Give me the pigeon, my dear, and I faithfully promise to show you where to find them.'

Hearing this, the lad was delighted beyond measure, and gave up the pigeon at once. Whereupon the white queen told him to seek her mother without delay, and ask for the eyes which she wore as a necklace.

'She will not fail to give them,' said the cruel queen, 'if you show her this token on which I have written what I want done.'

So saying, she gave the lad a piece of broken potsherd, with these words inscribed on it—'Kill the bearer at once, and sprinkle his blood like water!'

Now, as the son of seven queens could not read, he took the fatal message cheerfully, and set off to find the white queen's mother.

Whilst he was journeying he passed through a town, where every one of the inhabitants looked so sad, that he could not help asking what was the matter. They told him it was because the king's only daughter refused to marry; so when her father died there would be no heir to the throne. They greatly feared she must be out of her mind, for though every good-looking young man in the kingdom had been shown to her, she declared she would only marry one who was the son of seven mothers, and who ever heard of such a thing? The king, in despair, had ordered every man who entered the city gates to be led before the princess; so, much to the lad's impatience, for he was in an immense hurry to find his mother's eyes, he was dragged into the presence chamber.

No sooner did the princess catch sight of him than she blushed, and, turning to the king, said, 'Dear father, this is my choice!'

Never were such rejoicings as these few words produced. The inhabitants nearly went wild with joy, but the son of seven queens said he would not marry the princess unless they first let him recover his mothers' eyes. When the beautiful bride heard his story, she asked to see the potsherd, for she was very learned and clever. Seeing the treacherous words, she said nothing, but taking another similar-shaped bit of potsherd, she wrote on it these words—'Take care of this lad, giving him all he desires,' and returned it to the son of seven queens, who, none the wiser, set off on his quest.

Ere long he arrived at the hovel in the ravine where the white witch's mother, a hideous old creature, grumbled dreadfully on reading the message, especially when the lad asked for the necklace of eyes. Nevertheless she took it off, and gave it to him, saying, 'There are only thirteen of 'em now, for I lost one last week.'

The lad, however, was only too glad to get any at all, so he hurried home as fast as he could to his seven mothers, and gave two eyes apiece to the six elder queens; but to the youngest he gave one, saying, 'Dearest little mother! I will be your other eye always!'

After this he set off to marry the princess, as he had promised, but when passing by the white queen's palace he saw some pigeons on the roof. Drawing his bow, he shot one, and it came fluttering past the window. The white hind looked out, and lo! there was the king's son alive and well.

She cried with hatred and disgust, but sending for the lad, asked him how he had returned so soon, and when she heard how he had brought home the thirteen eyes, and given them to the seven blind queens, she could hardly restrain her rage. Nevertheless she pretended to be charmed with his success, and told him that if he would give her this pigeon also, she would reward him with the Jogi's wonderful cow, whose milk flows all day long, and makes a pond as big as a kingdom. The lad, nothing loath, gave her the pigeon; whereupon, as before, she bade him go and ask her mother for the cow, and gave him a potsherd whereupon was written—'Kill this lad without fail, and sprinkle his blood like water!'

But on the way the son of seven queens looked in on the princess, just to tell her how he came to be delayed, and she, after reading the message on the potsherd, gave him another in its stead; so that when the lad reached the old hag's hut and asked her for the Jogi's cow, she could not refuse, but told the boy how to find it; and, bidding him of all things not to be afraid of the eighteen thousand demons who kept watch and ward over the treasure, told him to be off before she became too angry at her daughter's foolishness in thus giving away so many good things.

Then the lad did as he had been told bravely. He journeyed on and on till he came to a milk-white pond, guarded by the eighteen thousand demons. They were really frightful to behold, but, plucking up courage, he whistled a tune as he walked through them, looking neither to the right nor the left. By and by he came upon the Jogi's cow, tall, white and beautiful, while the Jogi himself, who was king of all the demons, sat milking her day and night, and the milk streamed from her udder, filling the milk-white tank.

The Jogi, seeing the lad, called out fiercely, 'What do you want here?'

Then the lad answered, according to the old hag's bidding, 'I want your skin, for King Idra is making a new kettle-drum, and says your skin is nice and tough.'

Upon this the Jogi began to shiver and shake (for no Jinn or Jogi dares disobey King Idra's command), and, falling at the lad's feet, cried, 'If you will spare me I will give you anything I possess, even my beautiful white cow!'

To this the son of seven queens, after a little pretended hesitation, agreed, saying that after all it would not be difficult to find a nice tough skin like Jogi's elsewhere; so, driving the wonderful cow before him, he set off homewards. The seven queens were delighted to possess so marvellous an animal, and though they toiled from morning till night making curds and whey, besides selling milk to the confectioners, they could not use half the cow gave, and became richer and richer by the day.

Seeing them so comfortably off, the son of seven queens started off with a light heart to marry the princess; but when passing the white hind's palace he could not resist sending a bolt at some pigeons which were cooing on the parapet. One fell dead just beneath the window where the white queen was sitting. Looking out, she saw the lad hale and hearty standing before her, and grew whiter than ever with rage and spite.

She sent for him to ask how he had returned so soon, and when she heard how kindly her mother had received him, she nearly had a fit; however, she dissembled her feelings as well as she could, and, smiling sweetly, said she was glad to have been able to fulfil her promise, and that if he would give her this third pigeon, she would do yet more for him than she had done before, by giving him the million-fold rice, which ripens in one night.

The lad was of course delighted at the very idea, and, giving up the pigeon, set off on his quest, armed as before with a potsherd, on which was written, 'Do not fail this time. Kill the lad, and sprinkle his blood like water!'

But when he looked in on his princess, just to prevent her

becoming anxious about him, she asked to see the potsherd as usual, and substituted another, on which was written, 'Yet again give this lad all he requires, for his blood shall be as your blood!'

Now when the old hag saw this, and heard how the lad wanted the million-fold rice which ripens in a single night, she fell into the most furious rage, but being terribly afraid of her daughter, she controlled herself, and bade the boy go and find the field guarded by eighteen million demons, warning him on no account to look back after having plucked the tallest spike of rice, which grew in the centre.

So the son of seven queens set off, and soon came to the field where, guarded by eighteen million demons, the million-fold rice grew. He walked on bravely, looking neither to the right or left, till he reached the centre and plucked the tallest ear, but as he turned homewards a thousand sweet voices rose behind him, crying in tenderest accents, 'Pluck me too! Oh, please pluck me too!' He looked back, and lo! there was nothing left of him but a little heap of ashes!

Now as time passed by and the lad did not return, the old hag grew uneasy, remembering the message 'his blood shall be as your blood'; so she set off to see what had happened.

Soon she came to the heap of ashes, and knowing by her arts what it was, she took a little water, and kneading the ashes into a paste, formed it into the likeness of a man; then, putting a drop of blood from her little finger into its mouth, she blew on it, and instantly the son of seven queens started up as well as ever.

'Don't you disobey orders again!' grumbled the old hag. 'Or next time I'll leave you alone. Now be off, before I repent my kindness!'

So the son of seven queens returned joyfully to his seven mothers, who, by the aid of the million-fold rice, soon became the richest people in the kingdom. Then they celebrated their son's marriage to the clever princess with all imaginable pomp; but the bride was so clever, she would not rest until she had made known her husband to his father, and punished the wicked white witch. So she made her husband build a palace exactly like the one in which the seven queens had lived, and in which the white witch now dwelt in splendour. Then, when all was prepared, she bade her husband give a grand feast for the king.

Now the king had heard much of the mysterious son of seven queens, and his marvellous wealth, so he gladly accepted the invitation; but what was his astonishment when on entering the palace he found it was a facsimile of his own in every particular! And when his host, richly attired, led him straight to the private hall, where on royal thrones sat the seven queens, dressed as he had last seen them, he was speechless with surprise, until the princess, coming forward, threw herself at his feet, and told him the whole story.

Then the king awoke from his enchantment, and his anger rose against the wicked white hind who had bewitched him so long, until he could not contain himself. So she was put to death, and her grave ploughed over, and after that the seven queens returned to their own splendid palace, and everybody lived happily.

The Rainbow Bird and the Crocodile
and How People First Got Fire

Long ago in the Dreamtime there was an Old Man who could do one thing no one else could do. He knew how to make fire. He was clever with fire too. He could balance it on his head, juggle it in the air, breathe it out of his mouth. But he was very mean and would not share that fire with anyone. So everyone else was cold at night, had to eat their food raw and had no way to light themselves through the dark.

One day a Boy came up to the Old Man and said, 'Hey, Old Man. I'm tired of eating my food raw and being cold at night. Please, please will you show me how to make fire?'

And the Old Man said, 'Aaarrrgh! I'm boss for fire! I'm boss! If you want to make fire you've got to use bud-bud sticks. Now go away and leave me alone!'

The Boy ran off thinking, Bud-bud sticks, what are bud-bud sticks? He looked here, there, and everywhere for bud-bud sticks but when you're looking for something and you don't know what it is how are you going to find it? He couldn't find the bud-bud sticks so he came back to the Old Man and he said, 'Hey, Old Man! I've been looking everywhere for them bud-bud sticks but I can't find them. Please, will you show me how to make fire?'

But the Old Man goes, 'Aaarrrgh! I'm boss for fire! I'm boss! Now go away and leave alone!' And the Boy ran for it. He was frightened of that old man.

But after a little while the Old Man was thinking to himself, Oh dear. Maybe I growled at that boy too much. He's only a boy after all. So he called him back and said, 'Hey, youngfella! Come here, sit down and I'll tell you a story.' So the Boy cautiously came back, sat down, and the Old Man told him a story. Maybe one story, two story, three stories. Dreamtime stories.

Then the Old Man said, 'Now I've done something for you. You've gotta do something for me.' And you'll never guess what the Old Man asked the Boy to do. He said, 'I want you to take the nits out of my hair.'

Now the funny thing is, when someone's taking nits out of your hair it makes you all sleepy, all drowsy, and as the Boy was taking nits out of the Old Man's hair he began to nod off. And the Boy thought to himself, If that Old Man falls properly asleep I can sneak out and find the bud-bud sticks and make fire for myself. But I'd better make sure he's asleep first. So he called out and said, 'Old Man! Wake up! Wake up!'

But the Old Man said, 'I'm really tired. I want to go to sleep. Go away and leave me alone.' Then he fell asleep and began to snore.

And the Boy thought, Now is my chance. He crept out of the hut and there lying on the ground were two sticks, not much longer than a foot and as thick as a finger. One of them had a little hole halfway through on one side. And somehow or other the Boy knew that these were the bud-bud sticks and he knew what to do.

He laid the stick with the hole flat on the ground with one foot at each end. Then he put the other stick down into the little hole and began to twirl it between his fingers. He twirled and twirled with all his strength until at last smoke began to rise up from where the two sticks were rubbing together. Then he reached out for some dry grass, put it on the smoke and blew gently. Suddenly, 'pouff!' There was a bright orange flame. It was his first fire. He was really excited. He peeled off some bark from a stringy bark tree, tied it into a bunch and dipped it into the flame. At last he had it. His first flaming firestick.

Then the Boy had a mischievous idea. He thought to himself, That Old Man, he's been really mean to me. I'm going to pay him back! And he took his firestick and made a big circle of fire in the dry grass all the way round the Old Man's hut. Then he took his firestick and ran off into the bush.

Now the Old Man was lying there fast asleep when suddenly his nostrils started twitching with the smoke. He sat up, he opened his eyes and looked around. He was surrounded by leaping, crackling flames and he knew that if he stayed there he'd be burned to death. Then suddenly he remembered that about fifty metres away on the other side of the fire was a billabong.

So he gathered all of his strength together and then he ran through the fire. But as he ran . . . through . . . the fire . . . he turned . . . into . . . a crocodile! And his skin got all burned and blistered on his back, went all lumpy and bumpy. But he made it through to the other side of the fire and plunged sizzling into the cool waters of the billabong . . .

And ever since then the Crocodile has lived in wet places—in the swamps and lakes and rivers and billabongs. His fire has gone out now. In fact he's frightened of fire. But sometimes if you get close to old Crocodile—but don't get too close—when he opens his jaws you can still hear him say, 'I'm boss! I'm boss! I'm boss!'

As for the Boy, now he had a good idea. Now he decided to give fire to people so whenever they wanted to make fire all they had to do was to get the wood from any tree. So he ran round the bush putting fire into the heart of every tree. But as he ran . . . round . . . the bush . . . putting fire . . . into the heart . . . of every tree . . . suddenly his legs shrank . . . his shoulders sprouted feathers . . . and he turned into a bird. When he finished he plunged the firestick into his tail and there was a ripple of colour through his feathers and he turned into a Rainbow Bee-Eater.

And still to this day there are two tassels hanging from the tail of the Rainbow Bee-Eater, and the people say that those are the remains of the firestick that was placed there all those many, many years ago in the Dreamtime of Australia.

The Boy Pu-nia
and the King of the Sharks

On one side of the island there lived a great shark: Kai-ale-ale he was named; he was the King of the Sharks of that place, and he had ten sharks under him. He lived near a cave that was filled with lobsters. But no one dared to dive down, and go into that cave, and take lobsters out of it, on account of Kai-ale-ale and the ten sharks he had under him; they stayed around the cave night and day, and if a diver ventured near they would bite him and devour him.

There was a boy named Pu-nia, whose father had been killed by the sharks. Now after his father had been killed, there was no one to catch fish for Pu-nia and his mother; they had sweet potatoes to eat, but they never had any fish to eat with them. Often Pu-nia heard his mother say that she wished she had a fish or lobster to eat with the sweet potatoes. He made up his mind that they should have lobsters.

He came above the cave where the lobsters were. Looking down he saw the sharks—Kai-ale-ale and his ten sharks; they were all asleep. While he was watching them, they wakened up. Pu-nia pretended that he did not know that the sharks had wakened. He spoke loudly so that they would hear him, and he said, 'Here am I,

Pu-nia, and I am going into the cave to get lobsters for myself and my mother. That great shark, Kai-ale-ale, is asleep now, and I can dive to the point over there, and then go into the cave; I will take two lobsters in my hands, and my mother and I will have something to eat with our sweet potatoes.' So Pu-nia said, speaking loudly and pretending that he thought the sharks were still asleep.

Said Kai-ale-ale, speaking softly to the other sharks, 'Let us rush to the place where Pu-nia dives, and let us devour him as we devoured his father.' But Pu-nia was a very cunning boy and not at all the sort that could be caught by the stupid sharks. He had a stone upon his hand while he was speaking, and he flung it towards the point that he said he was going to dive to. Just as soon as the stone struck the water the sharks made a rush to the place, leaving the cave of the lobsters unguarded. Then Pu-nia dived. He went into the cave, took two lobsters in his hands, and came up on the place that he had spoken from before.

He shouted down to the sharks, 'Here is Pu-nia, and he has come back safely. He has two lobsters, and he and his mother have something to live on. It was the first shark, the second shark, the third shark, the fourth shark, the fifth shark, the sixth shark, the seventh shark, the eighth shark, the ninth shark, the tenth shark— it was the tenth shark, the one with the thin tail, that showed Pu-nia what to do.'

When the King of the Sharks, Kai-ale-ale, heard this from Pu-nia, he ordered all the sharks to come together and stay in a row. He counted them, and there were ten of them, and the tenth one had a thin tail. 'So it was you, Thin Tail,' he said, 'that told the boy Pu-nia what to do. You shall die.' Then, according to the orders of Kai-ale-ale, the thin-tailed shark was killed.

Pu-nia called out to them, 'You have killed one of your own kind.' With the two lobsters in his hands, he went back to his mother's.

Pu-nia and his mother now had something to eat with their sweet potatoes. And when the lobsters were all eaten, Pu-nia went back to the place above the cave. He called out, as he had done the first time, 'I can dive to the place over there and then slip into the cave, for the sharks are all asleep. I can get two lobsters for myself and my mother, so that we'll have something to eat with our sweet potatoes.' Then he threw down a stone and made ready to dive to another point.

When the stone struck the water the sharks rushed over, leaving the cave unguarded. Then Pu-nia dived down and went into the cave. He took two lobsters in his hands and swam back to the top of the water, and when he got to the place that he had spoken from before, he shouted down to the sharks, 'It was the first shark, the second shark, the third shark, the fourth shark, the fifth shark, the sixth shark, the seventh shark, the eighth shark, the ninth shark—it was the ninth shark, the one with the big stomach, that told Pu-nia what to do.'

Then the King of the Sharks, Kai-ale-ale, ordered the sharks to get into a line. He counted them, and he found that the ninth shark had a big stomach. 'So it was you that told Pu-nia what to do,' he said; and he ordered the big-stomached shark to be killed. After that Pu-nia went home with his two lobsters, and he and his mother had something to eat with their sweet potatoes.

Pu-nia continued to do this. He would deceive the sharks by throwing a stone to the place that he said he was going to dive to; when he got the sharks away from the cave, he would dive down, slip in, and take two lobsters in his hands. And always, when he got to the top of the water, he would name a shark.

'The first shark, the second shark, the third shark—the shark with the little eye, the shark with the grey spot on him—told Pu-nia what to do,' he would say; and each time he would get one of the sharks killed. He kept on doing this until only one of the sharks was left; this one was Kai-ale-ale, the King of the Sharks.

After that, Pu-nia went into the forest; he hewed out two hard pieces of wood, each about a yard long; then he took sticks for lighting a fire—the au-li-ma to rub with, and the au-na-ki to rub on; he got charcoal to burn as a fire, and he got food. He put all into a bag, and he carried the bag down to the beach. He came above the cave that Kai-ale-ale was watching, and he said, speaking in a loud voice, 'If I dive now, and if Kai-ale-ale bites me, my blood will come to the top of the water, and my mother will see the blood and will bring me back to life again. But if I dive down and Kai-ale-ale takes me into his mouth whole, I shall die and never come back to life again.'

Kai-ale-ale was listening, of course. He said to himself, 'No, I will not bite you, you cunning boy; I will take you into my mouth and swallow you whole, and then you will never come back to life again. I shall open my mouth wide enough to take you in. Yes, indeed, this time I will get you.'

Pu-nia dived holding his bag. Kai-ale-ale opened his mouth wide and got Pu-nia into it. But as soon as the boy got within, he opened his bag and took out the two pieces of wood which he had hewn out in the forest. He put them between the jaws of the shark so that Kai-ale-ale was not able to close his jaws. With his mouth held open, Kai-ale-ale went dashing through the water.

Pu-nia was now inside the big shark; he took the fire sticks out of his bag and rubbed them together, making a fire. He kindled the charcoal that he had brought, and he cooked his food at the fire that he had made. With the fire in his insides, the shark could not keep still; he went dashing here and there through the ocean.

At last the shark came near the Island of Hawaii again. 'If he brings me near the breakers, I am saved,' said Pu-nia, speaking aloud, 'but if he takes me to the sand near where the grass grows, I shall die; I cannot be saved.'

Kai-ale-ale, when he heard Pu-nia say this, said to himself, 'I will not take him near the breakers; I will take him where the dry sand is, near the grass.' Saying this, he dashed in from the ocean and up to where the shrubs grew on the shore. No shark had ever gone there before; and when Kai-ale-ale got there, he could not get back again.

Then Pu-nia came out of the shark. He shouted out, 'Kai-ale-ale, Kai-ale-ale, the King of the Sharks, has come to visit us.' And the people, hearing about their enemy Kai-ale-ale, came down to the shore with their spears and their knives and killed him. And that was the end of the ugly and wicked King of the Sharks.

Every day after that, Pu-nia was able to go down into the cave and get lobsters for himself and his mother. And all the people rejoiced when they knew that the eleven sharks that guarded the cave had been got rid of by the boy Pu-nia.

The Bones of Djulung

In a beautiful island that lies in the southern seas, where chains of gay orchids bind the trees together, and the days and nights are equally long and nearly equally hot, there once lived a family of seven sisters. Their father and mother were dead, and they had no brothers, so the eldest girl ruled over the rest, and they all did as she bade them. One sister had to clean the house, a second carried water from the spring in the forest, a third cooked their food, while to the youngest fell the hardest task of all, for she had to cut and bring home the wood which was to keep the fire continually burning. This was very hot and tiring work, and when she had fed the fire and heaped up in a corner the sticks that were to supply it till the next day, she often threw herself down under a tree, and went sound asleep.

One morning, however, as she was staggering along with her bundle on her back, she thought that the river which flowed past their hut looked so cool and inviting that she determined to bathe in it, instead of taking her usual nap. Hastily piling up her load by the fire, and thrusting some sticks into the flame, she ran down to the river and jumped in. How delicious it was diving and swimming and floating in the dark forest, where the trees were so thick that you could hardly see the sun! But after a while she began to look

65

about her, and her eyes fell on a little fish that seemed made out of a rainbow, so brilliant were the colours he flashed out.

I should like him for a pet, thought the girl, and the next time the fish swam by, she put out her hand and caught him. Then she ran along the grassy path till she came to a cave in front of which a stream fell over some rocks into a basin. Here she put her little fish, whose name was Djulung-djulung, and promising to return soon and bring him some dinner, she went away.

By the time she got home, the rice for their dinner was ready cooked, and the eldest sister gave the other six their portions in wooden bowls. But the youngest did not finish hers, and when no one was looking, stole off to the fountain in the forest where the little fish was swimming about.

'See! I have not forgotten you,' she cried, and one by one she let the grains of rice fall into the water, where the fish gobbled them up greedily, for he had never tasted anything so nice.

'That is all for today,' she said at last, 'but I will come again tomorrow,' and bidding him goodbye she went down the path.

Now the girl did not tell her sisters about the fish, but every day she saved half of her rice to give him, and called him softly in a little song she had made for herself. If she sometimes felt hungry, no one knew of it, and, indeed, she did not mind that much, when she saw how the fish enjoyed it. And the fish grew fat and big, but the girl grew thin and weak, and the loads of wood felt heavier every day, and at last her sisters noticed it.

Then they took counsel together, and watched her to see what she did, and one of them followed her to the fountain where Djulung lived, and saw her give him all the rice she had saved from her breakfast.

Hastening home the sister told the others what she had witnessed, and that a lovely fat fish might be had for the catching. So the eldest sister went and caught him, and he was boiled for supper, but the youngest sister was away in the woods, and did not know anything about it.

Next morning she went as usual to the cave, and sang her little song, but no Djulung came to answer it; twice and thrice she sang, then threw herself on her knees by the edge, and peered into the dark water, but the trees cast such a deep shadow that her eyes could not pierce it.

'Djulung cannot be dead, or his body would be floating on the surface,' she said to herself, and rising to her feet she set out homewards, feeling all of a sudden strangely tired.

What is the matter with me? she thought, but somehow or other she managed to reach the hut, and threw herself down in a corner, where she slept so soundly that for days no one was able to wake her.

At length, one morning early, a cock began to crow so loud that she could sleep no longer; and as he continued to crow she seemed to understand what he was saying, and that he was telling her that Djulung was dead, killed and eaten by her sisters, and that his bones lay buried under the kitchen fire. Very softly she got up, and took up the large stone under the fire, and creeping out carried the bones to the cave by the fountain, where she dug a hole and buried them anew. And as she scooped out the hole with a stick she sang a song, bidding the bones grow till they became a tree—a tree that reached up so high into the heavens that its leaves would fall across the sea into another island, whose king would pick them up.

As there was no Djulung to give her rice to, the girl soon became fat again, and as she was able to do her work as of old, her sisters did not trouble about her. They never guessed that when she went into the forest to gather her sticks, she never failed to pay a visit to the tree, which grew taller and more wonderful day by day. Never was such a tree seen before. Its trunk was of iron, its leaves were of silk, its flowers of gold, and its fruit of diamonds, and one evening, though the girl did not know it, a soft breeze took one of the leaves, and blew it across the sea to the feet of one of the king's attendants.

'What a curious leaf! I have never beheld one like it before. I must show it to the king,' he said, and when the king saw it he declared he would never rest until he had found the tree which bore it, even if he had to spend the rest of his life in visiting the islands that lay all around. Happily for him, he began with the island that was nearest, and here in the forest he suddenly saw standing before him the iron tree, its boughs covered with shining leaves like the one he carried about him.

'But what sort of tree is it, and how did it get here?' he asked of the attendants he had with him.

No one could answer him, but as they were about to pass out of the forest a little boy went by, and the king stopped and enquired if there was anyone living in the neighbourhood whom he might question.

'Seven girls live in a hut down there,' replied the boy, pointing with his finger to where the sun was setting.

'Then go and bring them here, and I will wait,' said the king, and the boy ran off and told the sisters that a great chief, with strings of jewels round his neck, had sent for them.

Pleased and excited the six elder sisters at once followed the boy, but the youngest, who was busy, and who did not care about strangers, stayed behind, to finish the work she was doing.

The king welcomed the girls eagerly, and asked them all manner of questions about the tree, but as they had never even heard of its existence, they could tell him nothing. 'And if we, who live close by the forest, do not know, you may be sure no one does,' added the eldest, who was rather cross at finding this was all that the king wanted of them.

'But the boy told me there were seven of you, and there are only six here,' said the king.

'Oh, the youngest is at home, but she is always half asleep, and is of no use except to cut wood for the fire,' replied they in a breath.

'That may be, but perhaps she dreams,' answered the king. 'Anyway, I will speak to her also.' Then he signed to one of his attendants, who followed the path that the boy had taken to the hut.

Soon the man returned, with the girl walking behind him. And as soon as she reached the tree it bowed itself to the earth before her, and she stretched out her hand and picked some of its leaves and flowers and gave them to the king.

'The maiden who can work such wonders is fitted to be the wife of the greatest chief,' he said, and so he married her, and took her with him across the sea to his own home, where they lived happy for ever after.

Tiger Story, Anansi Story

I. ANANSI ASKS A FAVOUR

Once upon a time, and a long, long time ago, all things were named after Tiger, for he was the strongest of all the animals, and King of the forest. The strong baboon, standing and smiting his chest like a drum, setting the trees ringing with his roars, respected Tiger and kept quiet before him. Even the brown monkey, so nimble and full of mischief, twisting the tail of the elephant, scampering about on the back of the sleeping alligator, pulling faces at the hippopotamus, even he was quiet before Tiger.

So, because Tiger ruled the forest, the lily whose flower bore red stripes was called tiger-lily, and the moth with broad, striped wings was called tiger-moth; and the stories that the animals told at evening in the forest were called Tiger Stories.

Of all the animals in the forest Anansi the spider was the weakest. One evening, looking up at Tiger, Anansi said, 'Tiger, you are very strong. Everyone is quiet in your presence. You are King of the forest. I am not strong. No one pays any attention to me. Will you grant me a favour, O Tiger?'

The other animals began to laugh. How silly of feeble Anansi to be asking a favour of Tiger! The bullfrog gurgled and hurried off to the pond to tell his wife how silly Anansi was. The green parrot in the tree called to her brother to fly across and see what was happening.

But Tiger said nothing. He did not seem to know that Anansi had spoken to him. He lay quiet, head lifted, eyes half closed. Only the tip of his tail moved.

Anansi bowed low so that his forehead almost touched the ground. He stood in front of Tiger, but a little to one side, and said, 'Good evening, Tiger. I have a favour to ask.'

Tiger opened his eyes and looked at Anansi. He flicked his tail and asked, 'What favour, Anansi?'

'Well,' replied Anansi in his strange, lisping voice, 'everything bears your name because you are strong. Nothing bears my name. Could something be called after me, Tiger? You have so many things named after you.'

'What would you like to bear your name?' asked Tiger, eyes half closed, tail moving slowly from side to side, his tawny, striped body quite still.

'The stories,' replied Anansi. 'Would you let them be called Anansi Stories?'

Now Tiger loved the stories, prizing them even more than the tiger-lily and the tiger-moth. Stupid Anansi, he thought to himself. Does he really think that I am going to permit these stories to be called Anansi Stories, after the weakest of all the animals in the forest? Anansi Stories indeed! He replied, 'Very well, Anansi. Have your wish, have your wish, but . . .'

Tiger fell silent. All the animals listened. What did Tiger mean, agreeing to Anansi's request and then saying 'but'? What trick was he up to? Parrot listened. Bullfrog stopped gurgling in order to catch the answer. Wise Owl, looking down from his hole in the trunk of a tree, waited for Tiger to speak.

'But what, Tiger? And it is so kind of you, Tiger, to do me this favour,' cried Anansi.

'But,' said Tiger, speaking loudly and slowly so that all might

71

hear, 'you must first do me two favours. Two favours from the weak equal one favour from the strong. Isn't that right, Anansi?'

'What two favours?' asked Anansi.

'You must first catch me a gourd full of live bees, Anansi. That is the first favour I ask of you.'

At this all the animals laughed so loudly that Alligator came out of a nearby river to find out what was happening. How could weak Anansi catch a gourd full of bees? One or two sharp stings would put an end to that!

Anansi remained silent. Tiger went on, eyes half closed. 'And there is a second favour that I ask, Anansi.'

'What is that, Tiger?'

'Bring me Mr Snake alive. Mr Snake who lives down by the river, opposite the clump of bamboo-trees. Both these things you must do within seven days, Anansi. Do these two small things for me, and I will agree that the stories might be called after you. It was this you asked, wasn't it, Anansi?'

'Yes, Tiger,' replied Anansi, 'and I will do these two favours for you, as you ask.'

'Good,' replied Tiger. 'I have often wished to sit and talk with Mr Snake. I have often wished to have my own hive of bees, Anansi. I am sure you will do what I ask. Do these two little things and you can have the stories.'

Tiger leapt away suddenly through the forest, while the laughter of the animals rose in great waves of sound. How could Anansi catch live bees and a live snake? Anansi went off to his home, pursued by the laughter of Parrot and Bullfrog.

II. THE FIRST TASK: A GOURD FULL OF BEES

On Monday morning Anansi woke early. He went into the woods carrying an empty gourd, muttering to himself. 'I wonder how many it can hold? I wonder how many it can hold?'

Ant asked him why he was carrying an empty gourd and talking to himself, but Anansi did not reply. Later, he met Iguana.

72

'What are you doing with that empty gourd?' asked Iguana. Anansi did not answer. Still further along the track he met a centipede walking along on his hundred legs.

'Why are you talking to yourself, Anansi?' asked Centipede, but Anansi made no reply.

Then Queen Bee flew by. She heard Centipede speaking to Anansi, and, full of curiosity, she asked, 'Anansi, why are you carrying that empty gourd? Why are you talking to yourself?'

'Oh, Queen Bee,' replied Anansi, 'I have made a bet with Tiger, but I fear that I am going to lose. He bet me that I could not tell him how many bees a gourd can hold. Queen Bee, what shall I tell him?'

'Tell him it's a silly bet,' replied Queen Bee.

'But you know how angry Tiger becomes, how quick-tempered he is,' pleaded Anansi. 'Surely you will help me?'

'I am not at all sure that I can,' said Queen Bee as she flew away. 'How can I help you when I do not know myself how many bees it takes to fill an empty gourd?'

Anansi went back home with the gourd. In the afternoon he returned to the forest, making for the logwood-trees, which at this time of the year were heavy with sweet-smelling yellow flowers and full of the sound of bees. As he went along he kept saying aloud, 'How many can it hold? How many can it hold?'

Centipede, who saw Anansi passing for the second time, told his friend Cricket that he was sure Anansi was out of his mind, for he was walking about in the forest asking himself the same question over and over again. Cricket sang the news to Bullfrog, and Bullfrog passed it on to Parrot, who reported it from his perch on the cedar-tree. Tiger heard and smiled to himself.

At about four o'clock that afternoon, Queen Bee, returning with her swarm of bees from the logwood-trees, met Anansi. He was still talking to himself. Well content with the work of the day, she took pity on him, and called out, 'Wait there, Anansi. I have thought of a way of helping you.'

'I am so glad, Queen Bee,' said Anansi, 'because I have been asking myself the same question all day and I cannot find the answer.'

'Well,' said Queen Bee, 'all you have to do is measure one of my bees, then measure your empty gourd, divide one into the other and you will have the answer.'

'But that's school-work, Queen Bee. I couldn't do that. I was never quick in school. That's too hard for me, too hard, Queen Bee. And that dreadful Tiger is so quick-tempered. What am I to do, Queen Bee?'

'I will tell you how to get the answer,' said one of the bees that advised the Queen. 'Really, it is quite easy. Hold the gourd with the opening towards the sunlight so that we can see it. We will fly in one at a time. You count us as we go in. When the gourd is full we will fly out. In this way you will find out the correct answer.'

'Splendid,' said Queen Bee. 'What do you think of that, Anansi?'

'Certainly that will give the answer,' replied Anansi, 'and it will be more correct than the school answer. It is a good method, Queen Bee. See, I have the gourd ready, with the opening to the sunlight. Ready?'

Slowly the bees flew in, their Queen leading the way, with Anansi counting, 'One, two, three, four, five . . . twenty-one, twenty-two, twenty-three . . . forty-one, forty-two, forty-three, forty-four,' until the gourd was half full, three-quarters full, '. . . a hundred and fifty-two, and fifty-three, and fifty-four.' At that point the last bee flew in, filling the gourd, now heavy with humming bees crowded together. Anansi corked up the opening and hurried off to the clearing in the forest where Tiger sat with a circle of animals.

'See, King Tiger,' he said, 'here is your gourd full of bees, one hundred and fifty-four of them, all full of logwood honey. Do you still want me to bring Brother Snake, or is this enough?'

Tiger was so angry that he could hardly restrain himself from leaping at Anansi and tearing him to pieces. He had been laughing with the other animals at Parrot's account of Anansi walking alone through the forest asking himself the same ridiculous question over and over. Tiger was pleased about one thing only, that he had set Anansi two tasks and not one. Well, he had brought the gourd full of bees. But one thing was certain. He could never bring Mr Snake alive.

'What a good thing it is that I am so clever,' said Tiger to himself. 'If I had set him only one task I would have lost the stories.' Feeling more content within himself, and proud of his cleverness, he replied to Anansi, who was bowing low before him, 'Of course, Anansi. I set you one thing that I knew you could do, and one that I know you cannot do. It's Monday evening. You have until Saturday morning, so hurry off and be gone with you.'

The animals laughed while Anansi limped away. He always walked like that, resting more heavily on one leg than on the others. All laughed, except Wise Owl, looking down from his home in the cedar-tree. The strongest had set the weakest two tasks.

Perhaps, thought Owl to himself, perhaps . . . perhaps . . .

III. THE SECOND TASK: MR SNAKE

On Tuesday morning Anansi got up early. How was he to catch Mr Snake? The question had been buzzing about in his head all night, like an angry wasp. How to catch Mr Snake?

Perhaps he could trap Snake with some ripe bananas. He would make a Calaban beside the path that Snake used each day when the sky beat down on the forest and he went to the stream to quench his thirst. How good a thing it is, thought Anansi, that Snake is a man of such fixed habits; he wakes up at the same hour each morning, goes for his drink of water at the same hour, hunts for his food every afternoon, goes to bed at sunset each day.

Anansi worked hard making his Calaban to catch Snake. He took a vine, pliant yet strong, and made a noose in it. He spread grass and leaves over the vine to hide it. Inside the noose he placed two ripe bananas. When Snake touched the noose, Anansi would draw it tight. How angry Mr Snake would be, to find that he had been trapped! Anansi smiled to himself while he put the finishing touches to the trap, then he hid himself in the bush by the side of the track, holding one end of the vine.

Anansi waited quietly. Not a leaf stirred. Lizard was asleep on the trunk of a tree opposite. Looking down the path Anansi could see heat waves rising from the parched ground.

There was Snake, his body moving quietly over the grass and dust, a long gleaming ribbon marked in green and brown. Anansi waited. Snake saw the bananas and moved towards them. He lay across the vine and ate the bananas. Anansi pulled at the vine to tighten the noose, but Snake's body was too heavy. When he had eaten the bananas Snake went on his way to the stream.

That was on Tuesday. Anansi returned home, the question still buzzing about in his head: 'How to catch Snake? How to catch Snake?' When his wife asked him what he would like for supper, he answered, 'How to catch Snake?' When his son asked if he could go off for a game with his cousin, Anansi replied, 'How to catch Snake?'

A Slippery Hole! That was the answer. Early on Wednesday morning he hurried back to the path in the forest where he had waited for Snake the day before, taking with him a ripe avocado pear. Snake liked avocado pears better even than bananas. In the middle of the path Anansi dug a deep hole, and made the sides slippery with grease. At the bottom he put the pear. If Snake went down into the hole he would not be able to climb back up the slippery sides. Then Anansi hid in the bush.

At noon Snake came down the path. 'How long he is,' said Anansi to himself; 'long and strong. Will I ever be able to catch him?'

Snake glided down the path, moving effortlessly until he came to the Slippery Hole. He looked over the edge of the hole and saw the avocado pear at the bottom. Also he saw that the sides of the hole were slippery. First he wrapped his tail tightly round the trunk of a slender tree beside the track, then lowered his body and ate the avocado pear. When he had finished he pulled himself out of the hole by his tail and went on his way to the river. Anansi had lost the bananas; now he had lost the avocado pear also!

On Wednesday Anansi spent the morning working at a 'Fly-Up', a trap he had planned during the night while the question buzzed through his head: 'How to catch Snake. How? How?' He arranged it cleverly, fitting one of the slender young bamboo-trees with a noose, so that the bamboo flew up at the slightest touch, pulling the noose tight. Inside the noose he put an egg, the only one that he had left. It was precious to him, but he knew that Snake loved eggs even more than he did. Then he waited behind the clump of bamboos. Snake came down the path.

The Fly-Up did not catch Snake, who simply lowered his head, took the egg up in his mouth without touching the noose, and then enjoyed the egg in the shade of the clump of bamboos while Anansi looked on. He had lost the bananas and avocado pear, and his precious egg.

There was nothing more to do. The question 'How to catch Snake?' no longer buzzed round and round in his head, keeping him awake by night, troubling him throughout the day. The Calaban, the Slippery Hole, and the Fly-Up had failed. He would have to go back to Tiger and confess that he could not catch Snake. How Parrot would laugh, and Bullfrog and Monkey!

Friday came. Anansi did nothing. There was no more that he could do.

Early on Saturday morning, before daybreak, Anansi set off for a walk by the river, taking his cutlass with him. He passed by the hole where Snake lived. Snake was up early. He was looking towards the east, waiting for the sun to rise, his head resting on the edge of his hole, his long body hidden in the earth. Anansi had not expected that Snake would be up so early. He had forgotten Snake's habit of rising early to see the dawn. Remembering how he had tried to catch Snake, he went by very quietly, limping a little, hoping that Snake would not notice him. But Snake did.

'You there, you, Anansi, stop there!' called Snake.

'Good morning, Snake,' replied Anansi. 'How angry you sound.'

'And angry I am,' said Snake. 'I have a good mind to eat you for breakfast.' Snake pulled half his body out of the hole. 'You have been trying to catch me. You set a trap on Monday, a Calaban. Lizard told me. You thought he was asleep on the trunk of the tree but he was not; and as you know, we are of the same family. And on Tuesday you set a Slippery Hole, and on Wednesday a Fly-Up. I have a good mind to kill you, Anansi.'

'Oh, Snake, I beg your pardon. I beg your pardon,' cried the terrified Anansi. 'What you say is true. I did try to catch you, but I failed. You are too clever for me.'

'And why did you try to catch me, Anansi?'

'I had a bet with Tiger. I told him you are the longest animal in the world, longer even than that long bamboo-tree by the side of the river.'

'Of course I am,' shouted Snake. 'Of course I am. You haven't got to catch me to prove that. Of course I am longer than the bamboo-tree!' At this, Snake, who was now very angry and excited, drew his body out of the hole and stretched himself out on the grass. 'Look!' he shouted. 'Look! How dare Tiger say that the bamboo-tree is longer than I am!'

'Well,' said Anansi, 'you are very long, very long indeed. But, Snake, now that I see you and the bamboo-tree at the same time, it seems to me that the bamboo-tree is a little longer than you are; just a few inches longer, Snake, half a foot or a foot at the most. Oh, Snake, I have lost my bet. Tiger wins!'

'Tiger, fiddlesticks!' shouted the enraged Snake. 'Anyone can see that the bamboo-tree is shorter than I am. Cut it down, you stupid creature! Put it beside me. Measure the bamboo-tree against my body. You haven't lost your bet, you have won.'

Anansi hurried off to the clump of bamboos, cut down the longest and trimmed off the branches.

'Now put it beside me,' shouted the impatient Snake.

Anansi put the long bamboo pole beside Snake. Then he said,

'Snake, you are very long, very long indeed. But we must go about this in the correct way. Perhaps when I run up to your head you will crawl up, and when I run down to see where your tail is you will wriggle down. How I wish I had someone to help me measure you with the bamboo!'

'Tie my tail to the bamboo,' said Snake, 'and get on with the job. You can see that I am longer!'

Anansi tied Snake's tail to one end of the bamboo. Running up to the other end, he called, 'Now stretch, Snake, stretch!'

Snake stretched as hard as he could. Turtle, hearing the shouting, came out of the river to see what was happening. A flock of white herons flew across the river, and joined in, shouting, 'Stretch, Snake, stretch.' It was more exciting than a race. Snake was stretching his body to its utmost, but the bamboo was some inches longer.

'Good,' cried Anansi. 'I will tie you round the middle, Snake, then you can try again. One more try, and you will prove you are longer than the bamboo.'

Anansi tied Snake to the bamboo, round the middle. Then he said, 'Now rest for five minutes. When I shout, "Stretch," then stretch as much as you can.'

'Yes,' said one of the herons. 'You have only six inches to stretch, Snake. You can do it.'

Snake rested for five minutes. Anansi shouted, 'Stretch.' Snake made a mighty effort. The herons and Turtle cheered Snake on. He shut his eyes for the last tremendous effort that would prove him longer than the bamboo.

'Hooray,' shouted the animals, 'you are winning, you are winning, four inches more, two inches more . . .'

At that moment Anansi tied Snake's head to the bamboo. The animals fell silent. There was Snake tied to the bamboo, ready to be taken to Tiger.

From that day the stories have been called Anansi Stories.

The Coming of Asin

There was once a chief among the Pilagá people by the name of Nalaraté. Nalaraté was known for his victories in war, and the men who followed him were battle-hardened warriors. Into Nalaraté's village one day there came a curious stranger. When the people saw him they laughed, for he was grotesque and ugly. Whereas other men were lean and straight, the stranger was crooked, with a large paunch. And whereas other men had long black hair, the stranger had none at all. Other men wore loincloths, but as for the stranger, he wore a fox-skin cloak over his shoulders.

'What kind of creature is this?' Nalaraté's people asked each other. 'He is not of the Toba tribe, nor of the Matacao, nor the Tereno. He must be a tribe all by himself, for where could there be other people like him?' They mocked him this way, but the stranger simply listened and made no answer. Finally one of the Pilagá asked him, 'Who are you?'

'My name is Asin,' the stranger answered quietly.

He remained in the village and built himself a small shelter of boughs and grass. The people tolerated him as a curiosity, and they treated him as a beggar. If a man caught a fish that was too small to cook, he might toss it to Asin, and Asin would take it humbly and express his thanks. But though the people didn't send Asin out of the village they abused him in many ways. Sometimes, for sport, the men would wipe their hands on Asin's fox-skin cloak and make a great joke of it when he complained.

One day Asin went to the house of the chief. Nalaraté said, 'Do not enter here. What is in my house that you want to steal?'

Asin answered, 'I only want to borrow a comb from your daughter.'

Nalaraté laughed. 'Since you have no hair on your head, what could you do with a comb?'

But Nalaraté's daughter overheard them talking, and she said to Asin, 'Here, I will lend you the comb.'

Asin took it and thanked her and went down to the river. The girl picked up her water jars and followed him, curious as to what he would do with a comb. When she came near the river, she hid among the trees and watched Asin. She saw him remove his fox-skin cloak. As Asin stood there in the water he changed instantly into a handsome young warrior with long black hair, which he combed with the comb the girl had lent him.

'He is handsome and he has great powers!' the girl said to herself. 'I will have him for my husband.'

Asin finished combing his hair. Then he transformed himself again into the ugly stranger, and put the fox-skin cloak back on his shoulders. After he had left, the girl filled her water jars and carried them home.

When Asin came to Nalaraté's house to return the comb, the girl said, 'Sit down with me here.'

Asin replied, 'Why do you want me to sit with you? I am ugly.'

The girl said, 'Even though my father will object, I will have you for my husband.'

Asin answered, 'Very well, then. Let us sit where people can see.'

The girl put a skin on the ground in front of the house and they sat on it together, signifying that they were married. When people saw them sitting there, they said, 'The chief's daughter has lost her mind. She is married to Asin.'

When Nalaraté came he was angry. He ordered his daughter to leave Asin and choose another man of the village, but she refused, saying, 'He is my husband now.'

That night, Asin demonstrated his magic powers. From under the fox-skin cloak he brought out a mosquito netting to protect them from insects. He brought out food, and they ate. He brought out a beautiful red skirt-cloth and gave it to his wife.

When the girl's mother saw what Asin could do, she said, 'I didn't protest when you married Asin. What can he bring out from under the fox skin for me?'

The girl said, 'Ask for whatever you want, he will give it to you.'

The mother said, 'It is the beautiful red skirt-cloth that I want.'

'Take it,' Asin said, and she took it. Then Asin reached under the fox-skin cloak and brought out a yellow skirt-cloth for his wife. He brought out ears of corn and a honeycomb full of honey and gave them to the girl's mother, and she was grateful. She said again, 'I wasn't one of those who objected to Asin's living here.'

Nalaraté was at a drinking party with the warriors of the village. When he returned early in the morning he said, 'Get my things ready, we are going on an expedition against the Matacao tribe.'

Asin said, 'I will come with you.'

The chief replied scornfully, 'No, how could I take you? You would be a hindrance. You are no warrior. You don't even have a horse. If you had a horse, could you even make it go in the right direction? And if you arrived at the place of battle, what could you do but cause us shame and misery? No, stay here with the women. As for my daughter, she chose a beggar instead of a warrior. She will starve. I will give her nothing.'

Nalaraté and his warriors mounted their horses and rode away. When they were out of sight, Asin said, 'Now I will go.'

He mounted his donkey and followed the war party. When he had left the village behind, he clapped his hands together, *tao*, and his donkey changed into a fiery iron horse. He clapped his hands again, *tao*, and changed himself into a handsome young man as his wife had seen him at the river. When night came, Nalaraté's warriors made camp. Before Asin entered the camp, he changed his iron horse back into a donkey, and himself into an ugly man without hair.

The war party saw him then, and they made jokes and asked, 'Why did you come?' They threw him some scraps of food, which he took. After a while he mounted his donkey and rode on ahead of the war party. He spent the night alone at a watering place. He brought out food from under his fox skin and he ate until he was satisfied.

In the morning he again joined the warriors, and he rode at a distance behind them. The men joked about Asin. Then they sighted the camp of the enemy. Nalaraté ordered Asin to return to the village. He said, 'Go back at once before you cause us trouble and shame.'

Asin stopped and waited, as the Pilagá men went cautiously forward. Then he changed himself into the warrior with the flowing black hair, and he changed his donkey into the fiery iron horse. He rode fiercely past the Pilagá men into the camp of the enemy and fought with them. Nalaraté's warriors stopped and watched the battle, asking each other, 'Who is this man? Who is this man?'

One of them cried out, 'It is Asin! He changed his donkey into a fiery iron horse!'

Then the Pilagá went forward to join the battle, but by the time they arrived Asin had scattered the enemy and rounded up all the horses. They met him coming back, driving the horses before him. He did not speak to the Pilagá, but went on and left them behind.

Asin returned to the village. He said to his wife, 'Let us leave this village where I have been mistreated.' His wife agreed. Her mother said, 'I will come too.' So Asin took them and his horses to a new place on the edge of a river and made a new house.

When Nalaraté arrived home he found his house empty. The women of the village told him how Asin had gone away with his household.

The men blamed Nalaraté, saying, 'It is your fault, you abused him. And he is the greatest of warriors.'

Nalaraté was angry. He said, 'If you want him for your chief, follow him.'

Many of the men did. They took their families and went to the place where Asin had built his house. There they built a new village. And Asin was the chief.

Nalaraté decided he would destroy Asin for the grief he had caused him. But Asin learned of the plot, and he called all the men of the village together and spoke to them. He said, 'There is a wind coming. It will be cold. Go and brace your houses, and put heavy thatch on the roof.' They went and prepared their houses. Then Asin clapped his hands, *tao*, and the cold wind came. It swept across the country. People became cold and sought refuge inside their houses. But the wind blew away the thatch from the roofs. Only in Asin's village did the roofs remain. Everywhere else people were punished by the cold and the wind. In his own house Asin clapped his hands, *tao*, and made a fire. People came to him begging for an ember so that they could have a fire in their houses too. To those people who were his friends, Asin gave firebrands. When his enemies came and begged for fire, he turned them away. Nalaraté himself came, but Asin said, 'First you merely abused me; then you planned to kill me. Why should I give you fire?' Nalaraté went away and was cold.

All those who hadn't abused Asin had fire and were warm, but the others suffered and died. The rivers froze, and snow covered the land.

At last the wind stopped, and the ice and snow melted, and Asin came out of his house. He went to Nalaraté's village and found the people dead. He changed the old men into yulo birds and mazamorras birds, and they flew away. He changed the old women into chaja birds, and they flew away. He changed the middle-aged people into hawks and vultures, and they flew away. And the children he changed into ducks and herons, and they flew away.

Asin found Nalaraté where he had taken refuge from the cold in a well, and he changed him into an alligator.

This is the legend of Asin, who was abused because of his appearance.

The Legend of the Yara

It is said that many years ago a young brave named Jaraguari lived on the banks of the Amazon River. This young man was as cheerful as the sun-dappled water of the great river, yet as strong and agile as the yellow-black jaguar, lord of the forest. He was the son of the chieftain of a small village. Each year, this village had a ceremony that celebrated a young man's rite of passage into the rank of warrior where manhood was honoured and a boy's skills as a hunter were tested. No more exquisite a hunter than Jaraguari had ever emerged. The villagers wondered at his boldness which surpassed that of all the other young braves who envied his courage and dexterity. None of them could approximate the uncanny precision with which he pierced the thick, hairy hide of a white-lipped peccary.

Jaraguari had in his keen eyes the strength of the great river. His disposition was as contented as the rhythmic waters that lapped along the shores of his village. The elders of the village loved Jaraguari because he treated them with kindness and respect. And the girls of the village dreamed at night of his handsome good looks, his grace, and his courage.

Paddling his canoe or *ubá* downriver with the prow barely disturbing the still waters, Jaraguari would set forth each day to fish, delighting in the skittish egrets that followed his trajectory. The river animals feared some of the braves because they fished by poisoning the waters with the sap from the deadly *timbó* plants. The poison killed the *piava*, the *pintado*, and the piranha fish. But the fish appreciated that Jaraguari would not poison them. Jaraguari would use one of his sharp arrows to spear the giant *pirarucu* fish.

He was nimble and elegant, and he respected the nobility of the many freshwater fish. When he returned each night at twilight, his mother would see him from the shore, standing proudly in the bow of his *ubá* surveying the day's catch.

Once a young man reached the rank of warrior, he was finally able to wear a necklace made from the teeth of the jaguars he had killed in the hunt. It was several moons after Jaraguari became a warrior that his mother glimpsed him returning very late one night. The stars were already dimming in the sky.

The next day Jaraguari seemed changed. He was pensive and reserved. Although his mother was concerned by his mood, he insisted on leaving that day at his usual hour, cutting the same route to Tarumã Point, where he remained until well past dusk. Each night thereafter, silent and solitary, he would return to shore, lost in his thoughts.

Astounded by the changes in her son, Jaraguari's mother finally asked him, 'What sort of fishing are you doing, my son, that goes on until so late an hour? Are you not afraid of the treacherous tricks of the jungle spirits? Have you never heard voices in the angry winds? Is that why you are so sad, my son?'

His mother's words were a warning to him. When she saw Jaraguari huddled in his hammock, staring into the dead of night, hour after mournful hour, contemplating the realm of darkness, she feared what might be happening to him. Jaraguari's response to her warning was silence.

'Son, where is the happiness that animated your life? Not long ago joy danced from your eyes. Now it has travelled to a place far from you and me.'

'Mother,' was all Jaraguari managed to say, in a voice so pathetic he could barely be heard.

Jaraguari's mother and the chieftain watched as their son, once so fresh and full of sap, withered away. He still accompanied his father on the hunting forays, and even in his present state he did not tremble at the scream of a puma. But as a day lengthened into dusk, he would abandon the young braves still setting snares and casting their nets, and return to his canoe. With great haste he would speed through the murky waters toward Tarumã Point.

Jaraguari's mother knew that in the great river there was believed to be the Yara, or the Spirit of the Water. A woman of unusual beauty, she had light pink skin, vivid eyes, and green-gold hair falling the length of her body. The Yara tormented the souls of the men who crossed her path by slowly drawing them to her irresistible songs. Her alluring power could fill the rivers with pink and red and deep purple light. It was well known that no warrior could withstand the Yara's enchantment. Whoever saw her was instantly attracted by her grace and charm. In fear of her power, when the sun began to set, the braves stayed away from lakes and rivers where she could be found singing her eerie melodies. The unfortunate beings who were captured by her haunting incantations and beauty were dragged down to the depths of the waters.

For this reason, Jaraguari's mother stood her ground, and, though her heart was heavy with forebodings, she berated her son. 'The evil water spirits have poisoned your soul. Your father and I want you to leave this village with us, and we will find a life where the bird of happiness will once again dance in your eyes.'

As if witnessing a marvellous spectacle, Jaraguari suddenly came to life, his eyes wide open. 'Mother, I saw her. I saw her swimming amidst the flowers, floating like the lilies in the lagoon. She is as beautiful as the moon in the clearest of skies. Mother, her hair is the colour of other worlds we know nothing of, and her face is pink like the rosy spoonbill feathers dusting the sullied plain. Her eyes are like two gem-stones, more fiery than the precious emerald, and her song hushes the roar of the waterfall so the river can hear her. When she looks into my eyes, I want to follow her to where the water divides and she descends to her home. There is nothing in the river a man will ever see more beautiful than the Yara. And I want to hear her song once more.'

Upon hearing her son's words, the alarmed mother threw herself on the ground, sobbing, and cried out to her son, 'Flee from this place, my son! Never again let your canoe reach Tarumā Point. You have seen the Yara. She is fatal. Run away, my son. Death will leap from her green eyes and kill you.'

The young man did not reply. He silently walked away from the village, already enchanted.

The next day, just as the *murucututú* birds flew from their day nest on the river's edge, Jaraguari's canoe glided quietly towards Tarumā Point, cleaving the darkening water. The lads fishing on the banks of the river saw him pass and cried out, 'Come, everyone, come and see Jaraguari!'

The women with water jars balanced atop their heads and all the little boys chasing crabs rushed to the promontory where in the distance Jaraguari's canoe could be seen cutting through the water towards the horizon. The horizon seemed to be fed by flames from the setting sun. The nearer the canoe came to the horizon's edge, the more it appeared ready to hurl itself into the emblazoned sky.

Standing beside the young warrior was a woman of such great beauty, it was as if she were aglow herself from something luminary within. Her pale pink limbs stood out as filigree cast in relief against the blood gleam of the disappearing sun. More stunning than her beauty was the colour of her long hair. As bright a green as parrot's plumage was the Yara's iridescent hair which shone like a halo of light around them both.

In the distance could be heard the screams of the braves and maidens. 'It's the Yara. The Yara!' they shouted as if in one voice.

They ran to the village and some could not resist looking back to see their chieftain's son traversing the night waters of the river into the realm of darkness.

The Hungry Peasant, God, and Death

Not far from the city of Zacatecas there lived a poor peasant, whose harvest was never sufficient to keep hunger away from himself, his wife and children. Every year his harvests grew worse, his family more numerous. Thus as time passed, the man had less and less to eat for himself, since he sacrificed a part of his own rations on behalf of his wife and children.

One day, tired of so much privation, the peasant stole a chicken with the determination to go far away, very far, to eat it, where no one could see him and expect him to share it. He took a pot and climbed up the most broken side of a nearby mountain. Upon finding a suitable spot, he made a fire, cleaned his chicken, and put it to cook with herbs.

When it was ready, he took the pot off the fire and waited impatiently for it to cool off. As he was about to eat it, he saw a man coming along one of the paths in his direction. The peasant hurriedly hid the pot in the bushes and said to himself, 'Curse the luck! Not even here in the mountains is one permitted to eat in peace.'

At this moment the stranger approached and greeted, 'Good morning, friend!'

'May God grant you a good morning,' he answered.

'What are you doing here, friend?'

'Well, nothing, señor, just resting. And, Your Grace, where are you going?'

'Oh, I was just passing by and stopped to see if you could give me something to eat.'

'No, señor, I haven't anything.'

'How's that, when you have a fire burning?'

'Oh, this little fire; that's just for warming myself.'

'Don't tell me that. Haven't you a pot hidden in the bushes? Even from here I can smell the cooked hen.'

'Well yes, señor, I have some chicken but I shall not give you any; I would not even give any to my own children. I came way up here because for once in my life I wanted to eat my fill. I shall certainly not share my food with you.'

'Come, friend, don't be unkind. Give me just a little of it!'

'No, señor, I shall not give you any. In my whole life I have not been able to satisfy my hunger, not even for one day.'

'Yes, you will give me some. You refuse because you don't know who I am.'

'I shall not give you anything, no matter who you are, I shall not give you anything!'

'Yes, you will as soon as I tell you who I am.'

'Well then, who are you?'

'I am God, your Lord.'

'Uh, hm, now less than ever shall I share my food with you. You are very bad to the poor. You only give to those whom you like. To some you give haciendas, palaces, trains, carriages, horses; to others, like me, nothing. You have never even given me enough to eat. So I shall not give you any chicken.'

God continued arguing with him, but the man would not even give Him a mouthful of broth, so He went His way.

When the peasant was about to eat his chicken, another stranger came along; this one was very thin and pale.

'Good morning, friend!' he said. 'Haven't you anything there you can give me to eat?'

'No, señor, nothing.'

'Come, don't be a bad fellow! Give me a little piece of that chicken you're hiding.'

'No, señor, I shall not give you any.'

'Oh yes, you will. You refuse me now because you don't know who I am.'

'Who can you be? God, Our Lord Himself, just left and not even to Him would I give anything, less to you.'

'But you will, when you know who I am.'

'All right; tell me then who you are.'

'I am Death!'

'You were right. To you I shall give some chicken, because you are just. You, yes, you take away the fat and thin ones, old and young, poor and rich. You make no distinctions nor show any favouritism. To you, yes, I shall give some of my chicken!'

The Spirit-Wife

A young man was grieving because the beautiful young wife whom he loved was dead. As he sat at the graveside weeping, he decided to follow her to the Land of the Dead. He made many prayer sticks and sprinkled sacred corn pollen. He took a downy eagle plume and coloured it with red earth colour. He waited until nightfall, when the spirit of his departed wife came out of the grave and sat beside him. She was not sad, but smiling. The spirit-maiden told her husband, 'I am just leaving one life for another. Therefore do not weep for me.'

'I cannot let you go,' said the young man, 'I love you so much that I will go with you to the land of the dead.'

The spirit-wife tried to dissuade him, but could not overcome his determination. So at last she gave in to his wishes, saying, 'If you must follow me, know that I shall be invisible to you as long as the sun shines. You must tie this red eagle plume to my hair. It will be visible in daylight, and if you want to come with me, you must follow the plume.'

The young husband tied the red plume to his spirit-wife's hair, and at daybreak, as the sun slowly began to light up the world, bathing the mountaintops in a pale pink light, the spirit-wife started to fade from his view. The lighter it became, the more the form of his wife dissolved and grew transparent, until at last it vanished altogether. But the red plume did not disappear. It waved before the young man, a mere arm's-length away, and then, as if rising and falling on a dancer's head, began leading the way out of the village, moving through the streets out into the cornfields, moving through a shallow stream, moving into the foot-hills of the mountains, leading the young husband ever westward towards the land of the evening.

The red plume moved swiftly, evenly, floating without effort over the roughest trails, and soon the young man had trouble following it. He grew tireder and tireder and finally was totally exhausted as the plume left him further behind. Then he called out, panting, 'Beloved wife, wait for me. I can't run any longer.'

The red plume stopped, waiting for him to catch up, and when he did so, hastened on. For many days the young man travelled, following the plume by day, resting during the nights, when his spirit-bride would sometimes appear to him, speaking encouraging words. Most of the time, however, he was merely aware of her presence in some mysterious way. Day by day the trail became rougher and rougher. The days were long, the nights short, and the young man grew wearier and wearier, until at last he had hardly enough strength to set one foot before the other.

One day the trail led to a deep, almost bottomless chasm, and as the husband came to its edge, the red plume began to float away from him into nothingness. He reached out to seize it, but the plume was already beyond his reach, floating straight across the canyon, because spirits can fly through the air.

The young man called across the chasm, 'Dear wife of mine, I love you. Wait!'

He tried to descend one side of the canyon, hoping to climb up the opposite side, but the rock walls were sheer, with nothing to hold on to. Soon he found himself on a ledge barely wider than a thumb, from which he could go neither forward nor back. It seemed that he must fall into the abyss and be dashed into pieces.

His foot had already begun to slip, when a tiny striped squirrel scooted up the cliff, chattering, 'You young fool, do you think you have the wings of a bird or the feet of a spirit? Hold on for just a little while and I'll help you.'

The little creature reached into its cheek pouch and brought out a little seed, which it moistened with saliva and stuck into a crack in the wall. With his tiny feet the squirrel danced above the crack, singing, '*Tsithl, tsithl, tsithl,* tall stalk, tall stalk, tall stalk, sprout, sprout quickly.' Out of the crack sprouted a long, slender stalk, growing quickly in length and breadth, sprouting leaves and tendrils, spanning the chasm so that the young man could cross over without any trouble.

On the other side of the canyon, the young man found the red plume waiting, dancing before him as ever. Again he followed it at a pace so fast that it often seemed that his heart would burst. At last the plume led him to a large, dark, deep lake, and the plume plunged into the water to disappear below the surface. Then the husband knew that the spirit land lay at the bottom of the lake. He was in despair because he could not follow the plume into the deep.

In vain did he call for his spirit-wife to come back. The surface of the lake remained undisturbed and unruffled like a sheet of mica. Not even at night did his spirit-wife reappear. The lake, the land of the dead, had swallowed her up. As the sun rose above the mountains, the young man buried his face in his hands and wept.

Then he heard someone gently calling: 'Hu-hu-hu,' and felt the soft beating of wings on his back and shoulders. He looked up and saw an owl hovering above him. The owl said, 'Young man, why are you weeping?'

He pointed to the lake, saying, 'My beloved wife is down there in the land of the dead, where I cannot follow her.'

'I know, poor man,' said the owl. 'Follow me to my house in the mountains, where I will tell you what to do. If you follow my advice, all will be well and you will be reunited with the one you love.'

The owl led the husband to a cave in the mountains and, as they entered, the young man found himself in a large room full of owl-men and owl-women. The owls greeted him warmly, inviting him to sit down and rest, to eat and drink. Gratefully he took his seat.

The old owl who had brought him took his owl clothing off, hanging it on an antler jutting out from the wall, and revealed himself as a manlike spirit. From a bundle in the wall this mysterious being took a small bag, showing it to the young man, telling him, 'I will give this to you, but first I must instruct you in what you must do and must not do.'

The young man eagerly stretched out his hand to grasp the medicine bag, but the owl drew back. 'Foolish fellow, suffering from the impatience of youth! If you cannot curb your eagerness and your youthful desires, then even this medicine will be of no help to you.'

'I promise to be patient,' said the husband.

'Well then,' said the owl-man, 'this is sleep medicine. It will make you fall into a deep sleep and transport you to some other place. When you awake, you will walk towards the Morning Star. Following the trail to the middle anthill, you will find your spirit-wife there. As the sun rises, so she will rise and smile at you, rise in the flesh, a spirit no more, and so you will live happily.

'But remember to be patient; remember to curb your eagerness. Let not your desire to touch and embrace her get the better of you, for if you touch her before bringing her safely home to the village of your birth, she will be lost to you forever.'

Having finished this speech, the old owl-man blew some of the medicine on the young husband's face, who instantly fell into a deep sleep. Then all the strange owl-men put on their owl coats and, lifting the sleeper, flew with him to a place at the beginning of the trail to the middle anthill. There they laid him down underneath some trees.

Then the strange owl-beings flew on to the big lake at the bottom of which the land of the dead was located. The old owl-man's magic sleep-medicine, and the feathered prayer sticks which the young man had carved, enabled them to dive down to the bottom of the lake and enter the land of the dead. Once inside, they used the sleep medicine to put to sleep the spirits who are in charge of that strange land beneath the waters. The owl-beings reverently laid their feathered prayer sticks before the altar of that netherworld, took up the beautiful young spirit-wife, and lifted her gently to the surface of the lake. Then, taking her upon their wings, they flew with her to the place where the young husband was sleeping.

When the husband awoke, he saw first the Morning Star, then the middle anthill, and then his wife at his side, still in deep slumber. Then she too awoke and opened her eyes wide, at first not knowing where she was or what had happened to her. When she discovered her lover right by her side, she smiled at him, saying: 'Truly, your love for me is strong, stronger than love has ever been, otherwise we would not be here.'

They got up and began to walk towards the pueblo of their birth. The young man did not forget the advice the old owl-man had given him, especially the warning to be patient and shun all desire until they had safely arrived at their home. In that way they travelled for four days, and all was well.

On the fourth day they arrived at Thunder Mountain and came to the river that flows by Salt Town. Then the young wife said, 'My husband, I am very tired. The journey has been long and the days hot. Let me rest here awhile, let me sleep a while, and then, refreshed, we can walk the last short distance home together.'

And her husband said, 'We will do as you say.'

The wife lay down and fell asleep. As her lover was watching over her, gazing at her loveliness, desire so strong that he could not resist it overcame him, and he stretched out his hand and touched her.

She awoke instantly with a start, and, looking at him and at his hand upon her body, began to weep, the tears streaming down her face. At last she said, 'You loved me, but you did not love me enough; otherwise you would have waited. Now I shall die again.' And before his eyes her form faded and became transparent, and at the place where she had rested a few moments before, there was nothing.

On a branch of a tree above him the old owl-man hooted mournfully, 'Shame, shame, shame.' Then the young man sank down in despair, burying his face in his hands, and ever after his mind wandered as his eyes stared vacantly.

If the young lover had controlled his desire, if he had not longed to embrace his beautiful wife, if he had not touched her, if he had practised patience and self-denial for only a short time, then death would have been overcome. There would be no journeying to the land below the lake, and no mourning for others lost.

But then, if there were no death, men would crowd each other with more people on this earth than the earth can hold. Then there would be hunger and war, with people fighting over a tiny patch of earth, over an ear of corn, over a scrap of meat. So maybe what happened was for the best.

Hankering for a Long Tail

One time, when the summertime had come and the hot sun liked to burn up everything, mosquito and sandfly and gnat, always buzzing, used their mouths too much and bothered Brer Rabbit too much. He didn't have anything to brush off the pests, so he began jumping around uselessly and soon ran out of breath.

So he went to scheming to see what he could do to get rid of them. He noticed Brother Bull Cow standing under a tree, chewing his cud in a satisfied way, and every time those bugs lit on him, Brother Cow switched his tail and knocked them, and they flew away and left him alone. Just then Brother Horse came along the road, and a fly buzzed around his haunches, and he just switched his tail and killed it dead.

Brother Rabbit was eating himself up with envy, vexed because he didn't have a long tail. He thought that when things like that were handed out he should have gotten a tail like they had. It made him mad to remember how he had been obliged to cry and beg with Sister Nanny Goat just to fool her into giving him even that stumpy little bit of cottontail he had now. There isn't any way in this world to take away the shame of having something that is nothing at all, like his stub of a tail. Fly and flea just buzz around, laughing at that poor excuse for a switch. A long tail would also have made a fine figure of a fellow! But there wasn't any way to go back to those times; the question he faced was how he was to get a sizeable tail right now.

He went home and he thought about it and thought about it until suddenly he hatched out a plan. It was a right bodacious plan too, but then Brer Rabbit is a right bodacious creature. There isn't anything so outrageous that he won't try to do it at least one time. And Brer Rabbit put on his store clothes, with his blue breeches and his yellow shoes, all fine. And he cocked his hat and took the path that went to Heaven to ask God if he wouldn't be so kind as to give him a long tail like those other creatures have.

It wasn't easy for Brer Rabbit to find the way because everybody he asked seemed to have a different notion about how to get there. Brer Rabbit listened to everyone and paid no attention to most of them, but kept a steady head about him and kept pushing on. And, by and by, it seemed as if the narrow path kind of rambled and rambled in front of him. And he went on and on until at last he was right at the front gate of Heaven and at the head of the long avenue of the Beautiful City. And he pushed in and walked along the grand boulevard and at last there he was, right in front of the Big House.

That house sure is big! Brer Rabbit had to walk a mile or more around the veranda to the back porch plaza. When he got there he took off his hat and he put it on the step. He took his bandana and dusted his yellow shoes and wiped his forehead and threw the rag into his hat. Then he reached over and knocked on the floor of the porch at the back door. Tap! Tap! Tap!—sort of easy-like.

His heart almost failed him, but nothing happened. He waited a little while. Then he rapped again. Maybe God isn't in—but no fresh tracks led away from the house. He decided to rap again, a little louder this time. And this time, God hollered out in the house in a great big voice, 'Who is there?' Brer Rabbit was really scared.

He said in a timid kind of whisper, 'It is me, sir.'

God eyeballed him and said, 'Who is me?'

'Well just me, Brer Rabbit, sir.'

And God asked mighty severely, 'What do you want, Brer Rabbit?'

'Just a little something, sir. Won't take you barely a minute to do it.'

'Humph! What sort of business are you up to now?' God said. 'Sit down and I'll be out right away.'

Brer Rabbit sat down on the steps. And after a long time while he mostly wished he had never come, God finally came out. The first look Brer Rabbit had of God, he was so scared that he almost took off and ran away. But when he thought about how badly he wanted that long tail he held his ground.

He jumped off the step and displayed his best manners, pulling his forelock and scraping the gravel with his feet. 'Now, Brer Rabbit,' God said, sort of gruffly, 'what is the thing that you want so badly that you have gotten bold enough to come way up here like this?'

Brer Rabbit pulled his forelock again and answered, 'Master, this weather is so hard on us poor creatures, I don't see how we survive. Looks like Brer Mocking Bird is the only one that can enjoy himself, and he has to go away out to the top of a tree in the woods before he can jump around and sing the way he does. We who have to stay on the ground have Satan's own time. Every sort of devilish biting and stinging and troubling thing just trying to stay alive, we have to contend with. The gnats, and green head flies, and sandflies, and the redbugs, and the ticks, and the chiggers, and all kinds of varmints like that bother us from first day clean to dark. They work from can to can't, and they work faithfully! And when darkness comes and they leave off, the mosquitoes and the gallinippers join hands to take their place and suck out blood and annoy us until the first day brings its light.

'Even then, Master, some creatures make out better than the rest because they have a real tail, not just a leftover stump like Sister Nanny Goat gave me. I noticed what nice tails Brother Bull Cow and Brother Horse were given. When a fly bothers them, all they have to do is wave their tails in the air and the flies and the mosquitoes are scared if they don't fly off. *Ping!* That long tail cracks down and they are dead. Now, sir'—Brer Rabbit got mighty bold and brash, but his voice came out as sweet as molasses—'I just came here to ask you to do something for me, Master! Please, sir, if you could be so kind as to give me a long tail so that I can brush away those pesky critters too.'

God cast his eyes down at Brer Rabbit and squinched up his forehead and looked him over. Then he puckered up his mouth like he had been biting a green persimmon. And he said, 'You are made like you are made. You have been contrary about that tail from the first day. Sister Nanny Goat did just as I told her, and she was kind to give you any tail at all. Even with all the blessings you already have you come here to me to get a tail like the very best of creatures have. Hmm! You are mighty little to have a long tail. Brother Horse and Brother Bull Cow are big and stand high off the ground, but your belly mostly drags in the dust. You can jump around in the grass to keep those flies off.'

'That's what I have been doing, sir, but it just wears me out.'

God looked at him closely. 'You just want to be in high fashion, don't you?'

'Who, sir? Why do I have to think about fashion, sir! I am thankful for what I have got. The flies are the only thing that brought me here!' But Brer Rabbit was so scared he couldn't keep from trembling just a little bit.

God kind of smiled at him and then sort of squinched up his face. 'Well, you are smart enough to get here, and that is more than most, so I reckon I'll set you a task to see just how smart you are. That will keep you from bothering me for a while. And if you do it, I might give you a long tail.'

With that he turned around and went into the house. He came right back out again with something in his hand.

Brer Rabbit jumped up from where he had been sitting and became polite again. God gave him a crocus bag and said, 'Take this bag and bring it back to me full of blackbirds.'

Poor Brer Rabbit cried out at that. But God looked sour at him, cocking his eye, and Brer Rabbit shut up.

Then God gave him a hammer and said, 'Knock out Brother Alligator's eye teeth with this hammer and fetch them to me.'

This time Brer Rabbit was so upset that he could only grunt.

Last, God took a little calabash and said, 'This you must fill with Brother Deer's eye water. You understand? Now, you get away from here. And don't come back bothering me until you have done the whole lot.' Then he turned on his heel and went back in the house and slammed the door.

Brer Rabbit felt so cut down to size that he could scarcely pick up his hat to put on his head and go home. His heart was heavy and he dragged his feet along the ground. He walked along and he thought. He shook his head and he thought. How could he catch blackbirds by the sackful? He wasn't a hawk! Why would anyone with good sense go anywhere near Brother Alligator's mouth—so how could he knock out his teeth with a hammer?

And getting Brother Deer's tears! Brother Deer is so foolish and skittery, if you just ask him about anything he gets scared and runs off. God fixed it so that it's mighty hard to get a long tail. It didn't look like he was ever going to get his.

Now, you know, Brer Rabbit is little, but he is as quick as a whip. And he worked his mind day and night on how to get a sack full of blackbirds. At last he figured out a scheme. During the fall, the white folks burn off the rice-field bank where the grass grows all summer and stands heavy. The fire just goes along, and the smoke rolls along ahead of it, and then all the birds living in the grass get foolish about the smoke and fly about like crazy.

So when they started that year, Brer Rabbit went down on the bank and got a big clump of grass, just a little way in front of where they were beginning to burn. And when the fire came that way and the heavy smoke reached them, the birds flew around madly, lighting on one bush and then another, just running away. At last they came down right in front of Brer Rabbit's clump of grass. He jumped out and caught a bird and put it in the sack, and he jumped around again and caught some more. The birds were so slippery he got his sack full at last, and he was very proud.

Next, he began to think about the problem of Brer Alligator's teeth. One fine day, he got his fiddle and he went down to the rice field by the river. Now Brer Rabbit worked the fiddle in his own devilish way at all the dances and picnics in the country, and made people lose their religion. And a whole lot of them had been turned out of their churches because they had crossed their feet to his dancing tunes, because when Brer Rabbit played, there aren't any feet around that can take any notice whether they are crossing or not!

Now, this day, Brer Rabbit sat down on a stump and started to play and sing and pat his foot. And when he did that something began to move, because he knew no animal could resist that music, expecially Brer Alligator. Brer Alligator, who was way down at the bottom of the river, yelled at him and came to the top of the water, poked his big eyes out, and looked about to see who it was playing like that. But Brer Rabbit didn't pay any attention to him. He sang and he played and he patted his foot.

Right away that music started to pull Brer Alligator out of the water, and he swam over to the bank. Still Brer Rabbit didn't pay any attention to him. He went on singing and playing and patting his foot just like no one was around.

Brer Alligator crawled out on the edge of the marsh and then climbed right up on the bank and sat down by Brer Rabbit; he popped his eyes up at him and listened.

Brer Rabbit stopped at last. Brer Alligator praised him to the sky for his singing and fiddling. Then he asked Brer Rabbit, 'Can you teach me how to play like that? I sure would like to play and sing like that, yes sir!'

Brer Rabbit made like he was thinking a little while and then said to him, 'Can't say about the singing because it depends on how a man's mouth is made if he can learn to sing or not.'

'Look in my mouth, Brer Rabbit, and tell me if it is right.' Brer Rabbit pretended like he didn't care. He told him it was hard to teach anyone to sing anyway. 'Do, Brer Rabbit!' he begged him. But Brer Rabbit pretended like he hadn't heard him. He just kind of scratched his head and started to hum a tune.

'Brer Rabbit! Man! You've got to stop that just for a minute. Look and see if I have the kind of mouth that you can teach how to sing,' Brer Alligator kept on begging.

Brer Rabbit just yawned and stretched himself and looked down at Brother Alligator, shaking his head and making clucking sounds.

'All right, then, maybe I can, but you have to listen to me close and do just as I say.'

'Sure! Sure! Brer Rabbit. Anything you say!'

'Then shut your eyes tight till I tell you to open them again.'

Brer Alligator shut them. 'Open your mouth wide—real wide —and hold it that way.' And Brer Alligator did just as he was told.

Brer Rabbit grabbed a little lightwood knot, and he jammed it into Brer Alligator's jaws to keep them wide open, clear back by the corners of Alligator's mouth, so he couldn't shut it down. And he said, 'Bite on that a minute and hold still.'

Then he whipped out his little hammer that God had given him and—*Crack! Crack!* He knocked out both of Brer Alligator's eye teeth. And then just as quickly he ran off with them.

Brer Alligator hollered and yelled and thrashed around looking for Brer Rabbit. But Brer Rabbit didn't pay any attention to him. He just scampered on home. And every time he thought how Brother Alligator's jaws might have scrunched down on him, he had to wiggle himself to feel if he was all there. Brer Rabbit was mighty satisfied with himself then, yes sir.

The last thing Brer Rabbit had to do was to get that calabash full of Brother Deer's eye water, and then he would have all the tasks done. But he knew that getting the eye water would be the hardest task of all. He could hardly sleep again because he was so bothered by the problem. He couldn't think of anything except to ask Brer

Deer directly to help him. But that wasn't any use because Brer Deer knew Brer Rabbit too well and would figure out that he was going to play some kind of trick on him. Deer would take off so fast when he saw Brer Rabbit that no one would even be able to catch up with him to argue the point.

The problem got so hard Brer Rabbit almost gave up the whole thing, but then he saw Brer Horse and Brother Bull Cow with their nice long tails switching and swinging and it reminded him of how fine he would look, walking on the Big Road, if he just had one of those long tails. He could sure sashay along the road and shake that tail about and just look so handsome. So he began to scratch his head again and think about it some more. Man, he is a schemer, that Brer Rabbit! And finally he got a notion.

Brer Deer lived way down deep in the woods. A long time ago, he used to live in the settlement. He and Brer Dog even planted land together. But Brother Deer, or one of the family, had a fight with Brer Dog; and what with one thing or another it got to be such a goings-on that Brer Dog and his family made Brer Deer and his family run away every time they got a chance. That's what made Brer Deer begin a little place way off by himself. Poor Brer Deer was scared of nearly all the animals because of that experience; in fact, he was the most frightened creature in the woods.

Brer Rabbit counted on that, and he went deep in the woods till he came to a little clearing where Brer Deer had his house. And he found Brer Deer lying down in the hot sun in his yard. Brer Rabbit passed the time of day with him. They talked a little bit about crops and weather and who had been turned out of church, and who had gotten killed at the picnic, and such things.

At last Brer Rabbit said, 'Brer Deer, you know I am your friend, right?'

'Sure, Brer Rabbit, I know that well.'

'You know I always do stick up for you, right?'

'Yes, man!'

'Very well, then, I have to inform you that they have been

throwing your name about so much up in the settlement that I had to come and tell you about it.'

'What! What did they say?'

'They said that you are no good at jumping any longer—that Sister Nanny Goat takes the prize for jumping nowadays.'

'Now! Brer Rabbit—who could say that? Why, I can jump three times higher than that no-count little thing!'

'Brer Dog said you couldn't, and I told him that just wasn't so. And I came here to give you the chance to show me how you can still jump higher than anyone. Now I saw Sister Nanny Goat jump a bush almost as high as that one over there, and she could jump it good, too. Can you jump that high?'

Brer Deer sucked his teeth and shook his head and just kind of smiled. He said, 'Man! When I was a little fellow, before I could ever walk, I could jump bushes like that one.'

'Well then, why don't you go on? That bush goes awful high up in the air for anyone to jump! But if you can make it, I would sure like to see it, so I could pass the word along in the street to Brer Dog.'

Brer Deer got up and he ran down his yard and then he came back over the bush just high and fine and graceful. Brer Rabbit looked astonished. He whistled. He slapped his leg praising Brer Deer for how high and far he could jump. 'That isn't anything,' said Brer Deer, and he jumped over another bush a little higher, just to show what he could do.

Brer Rabbit loudly sang out his praises. 'Brer Dog is sure going to have to shut his lying mouth now when I carry the tale to everyone about how fine you jump. Man! you look nice doing that! I reckon you could even jump that big bush yonder?'

And Brer Deer took that one as well. So Brer Rabbit pointed to higher and higher bushes, till at last he fixed on one that wasn't a bush—it was more like a young tree, and it had a heavy fork and was all tangled up with jasmine and cat briar and snailox and supplejack and other kinds of vines.

When he looked at the tree with jasmine, Brother Deer sort of hesitated. But Brother Rabbit encouraged him with so much praise that he reared back and jumped it. He leaped very high in the air— but he didn't quite make it. He landed slam bang right in the middle in the big fork!

The jump knocked his breath out of him. When he twisted around to get out, he got so tangled up in that jacktwine and briar that it got harder to move. He hollered for Brer Rabbit to come help him.

Brer Rabbit made sure that he was caught fast and he said, 'Man, I can't help you. You're too heavy and you might fall on me and bust my back. But I will go right away to the settlement and find some help to get you out.'

With that, he ran down the path until he was out of sight and then he threw himself on the ground and he rolled and cackled and laughed at the way he had fooled Brer Deer and the way he was going to get his way now. Brer Rabbit laughed till he was crying.

And then he got up off the ground and pulled his handkerchief out of his pocket and ran back to Brer Deer wailing and sobbing. 'Brer Deer, you better get out of that bush now. Don't waste a minute because Brother Dog—' And he made out like he couldn't speak, he was crying so.

'What's the matter, Brer Rabbit?' Brer Deer was so scared that his voice trembled.

'You better come out right now because Brother Dog and his whole family are right behind me, and they're going to kill you and eat you if you stay in that bush. When I got close to the settlement, I saw them running down the path coming this way.'

Brer Deer shook and kicked himself. He pulled and he pushed but all he did was tangle himself more tightly in the jacktwine. 'Get out of that bush, Brer Deer! Get out of that bush before they get here and kill you right in front of my eyes.' And Brer Rabbit bowed his head and mopped his eyes with his handkerchief.

Then Brother Deer burst out crying. He struggled and cried, and then he struggled and then he cried some more. And all that time Brother Rabbit made out as if he was helping him out, but all he was doing was tangling the vines around Brother Deer's foot. Then he held out that little calabash that God had given him and caught every drop of that eye water which ran out of Brer Deer's eyes.

Every time Brer Deer looked like he might let up, Brer Rabbit screeched out, 'Oh, poor Brother Deer! You are going to be caught today!' And Brer Deer would bawl out some more.

But even so, the calabash wasn't quite full yet, so Rabbit called out, 'I see them getting closer, Brer Deer, howling for your meat! Hurry, Brer Deer, and get loose, or no one can save you!'

Brer Deer struggled the best he could, but he couldn't move himself and he went on crying. And so with all of that Brer Rabbit filled the calabash with eye water. Then he picked up the little calabash and he wiped his own eyes and he didn't say anything else. He just walked away and left Brer Deer high up in the tree fork.

Now that Brer Rabbit was all done with the tasks God had given him, he didn't waste any time. He went home, put on his store clothes, and picked up the three things that God had asked for. He took the path to God's house and all the way he swaggered.

When he got there this time he didn't go to any back door, no sir! He walked right up to the front door, and knocked bold and loud. *BAM! BAM! BAM!*

God was in the house and hollered out, 'Who is there?'

And Brer Rabbit answered, 'It's me, sir, Brer Rabbit!'

'What?' God's voice sounded kind of curious. 'You're back already, are you? You haven't done all the tasks I set you to do?'

'Yes, sir.'

'You mean to tell me you got all those things I told you to get?'

'Yes, sir. They are all right here, sir.'

'Take care with your foolishness, Brother Rabbit! You don't lie to me?'

'No, sir. I have them all, sir.'

God didn't make any sound for a while, but after such a length of time he came out to the door. Brer Rabbit kind of puffed himself up. He felt so pleased with himself that he was just grinning all over his face. Then he noticed that God looked vexed. And Brer Rabbit straightened up his face, put down the sack of blackbirds, then reached down in his side pocket and pulled out a little handkerchief and unwrapped Brer Alligator's two eye teeth, and handed them to God. There they were for sure, and the blood was still on them. And he hunted in his coat-tail pocket and pulled out the calabash full of Brother Deer's eye water.

God tasted it, and smelt it, and then he said, 'You are smart, aren't you, Brother Rabbit! Very well, then!' He pointed to a loblolly pine tree out in the yard. 'You go and seat yourself underneath that pine tree till I can fix you up.' And he turned around and went into the house and slammed the door after him. *BAM!*

Now Brer Rabbit went and did as he was told and sat down under that tree. But he didn't like the way God had slammed the door at all. And he didn't like the way God had talked to him. And he noticed that God's eyes showed red like fire when he looked at the pine tree. And Brer Rabbit couldn't rest easy because he was getting more and more scared. He scuffled around on his haunches—little bit by little bit—till he got to the other side of the tree trunk from the Big House, and sneaked away real quietly, keeping the tree between him and the house, till he got away over in the corner of the yard where he could hide himself under a heavy sucklebush.

Well, sir! He was hardly in the sucklebush before, *BRAM! BRAM! BRAM!* Out of the clear sky that didn't have so much as a cloud in it came the biggest thunder and lightning bolt that ever was seen. Wow! It just crashed down on the loblolly where Brer Rabbit had been! And the next minute, where that pine tree stood, there wasn't anything at all except a pile of kindling, and that was afire. Brer Rabbit didn't stop for anything! He took his feet in his hands and hit the avenue to the Big Gate and he screamed.

About that time, God in the Big House looked out of the window and saw a little something just running lickety-split down the avenue. And he looked close and sure enough it was Brother Rabbit. He leaned out of the window and put his two hands to his mouth and he hollered: 'Ah-hah! Ah-hah! Ah-hah! You think you are so smart, eh! You are so drat smart! Well, get a long tail yourself.'

The Two Old Women's Bet

One time there were two old women got to talkin' about the menfolks: how foolish they could act and what was the craziest fool thing their husbands had ever done. And they got to arguin', so finally they made a bet which one could make the biggest fool of her husband.

So one of 'em said to her man when he come in from work that evenin', says, 'Old man, do you feel all right?'

'Yes,' he says, 'I feel fine.'

'Well,' she told him, 'you sure do look awful puny.'

Next mornin' she woke him up, says, 'Stick out your tongue, old man.' He stuck his tongue out, and she looked at it hard, says, 'Law me! You better stay in the bed today. You must be real sick from the look of your tongue.'

Went and reached up on the mantelpiece, got down all the bottles of medicine and tonic was there and dosed the old man out of every bottle. Made him stay in the bed several days, and she kept on talkin' to him about how sick he must be. Dosed him every few minutes and wouldn't feed him nothin' but mush.

Came in one mornin', sat down by the bed, and looked at him real pitiful, started in snifflin' and wipin' her eyes on her apron, says, 'Well, honey, I'll sure miss ye when you're gone.' Sniffed some more, says, 'I done had your coffin made.'

And in a few days she had 'em bring the coffin right on in beside the old man's bed. Talked at the old man till she had him thinkin' he was sure 'nough dead. And finally they laid him out, and got everything fixed for the buryin'.

Well, the day that old woman had started a-talkin' her old man into his coffin, the other'n she had gone on to her house and about the time her old man came in from work she had got out her spinnin' wheel and went to whirlin' it. There wasn't a scrap of wool on the spindle, and the old man he finally looked over there and took notice of her, says, 'What in the world are ye doin', old woman?'

'Spinnin',' she told him, and 'fore he could say anything she says, 'Yes, the finest thread I ever spun. It's wool from virgin sheep, and they tell me anybody that's been tellin' his wife any lies can't see the thread.'

So the old man he come on over there and looked at the spindle, says, 'Yes, indeed, hit surely is mighty fine thread.'

Well, the old woman she'd be there at her wheel every time her old man come in from the field—spin and wind, spin and wind, and every now and then take the shuck off the spindle like it was full of thread and lay it in a box. Then one day the old man come in and she was foolin' with her loom, says, 'Got it all warped off today. Just got done threadin' it on the loom.' And directly she sat down and started in weavin'—step on the treadles, throwin' the shuttle and it empty. The old man he'd come and look and tell her what fine cloth it was, and the old woman she'd weave right on. Made him think she was workin' day and night. Then one evenin' she took hold on the beam and made the old man help her unwind the cloth.

'Lay it on the table, old man—Look out! You're a-lettin' it drag the floor.'

Then she took her scissors and went to cuttin'.

'What you makin', old woman?'

'Makin' you the finest suit of clothes you ever had.'

Got out a needle directly and sat down like she was sewin'. And there she was, every time the old man got back to the house, workin' that needle back and forth. So he come in one evenin' and she says to him, 'Try on the britches, old man. Here.' The old man he shucked off his overalls and made like he was puttin' on the new britches.

'Here's your new shirt,' she told him, and he pulled off his old one and did his arms this-a-way and that-a-way gettin' into his fine new shirt. 'Button it up, old man.' And he put his fingers up to his throat and fiddled 'em right on down.

'Now,' she says, 'let's see does the coat fit ye.' And she come at him with her hands up like she was holdin' out his coat for him, so he backed up to her and stuck his arms in his fine new coat.

'Stand off there now, and let me see is it all right—Yes, it's just fine. You sure do look good.'

And the old man stood there with nothin' on but his shoes and his hat and his long underwear.

Well, about that time the other old man's funeral was appointed and everybody in the settlement started for the buryin' ground. The grave was all dug and the preacher was there, and here came the coffin in a wagon, and finally the crowd started gatherin'. And pretty soon that old man with the fine new suit of clothes came in sight. Well, everybody's eyes popped open, and they didn't know whether they ought to laugh or not, but the kids went to gigglin' and about the time that old man got fairly close, one feller laughed right out, and then they all throwed their heads back and laughed good. And the old man he'd try to tell somebody about his fine new suit of clothes, and then the preacher busted out laughin' and slappin' his knee—and everybody got to laughin' and hollerin' so hard the dead man sat up to see what was goin' on. Some of 'em broke and ran when the corpse rose up like that, but they saw him start in laughin'—laughed so hard he nearly fell out the coffin—so they all came back to find out what-'n-all was goin' on.

The two old women had started in quarrellin' about which one had won the bet, and the man in the coffin heard 'em, and when he could stop laughin' long enough, he told 'em, says, 'Don't lay it on me, ladies! He's got me beat a mile!'

Jean Labadie's Dog

Jean Labadie stood in the chicken yard and counted chickens. 'If the weasels aren't getting my chickens,' Jean Labadie said, 'you can bet your life my good neighbour André Drouillard is getting them.'

Jean Labadie decided he would catch André Drouillard in the act of absconding with his poultry. So for three nights he slept in the chicken yard with his shotgun by his side. But nothing happened. André's sixth sense must have warned him.

Jean Labadie got tired of sleeping with the chickens, and he went back to sleeping in the house. But he was determined to do something about the chicken stealing. The only thing was, he didn't know what. You can't just ask a man if he's stealing your chickens, even if he is. Therefore, Jean Labadie didn't do anything for a while.

Then one day he was helping André Drouillard clear the brushwood along the fences. While he was working, he found a pile of chicken feathers. Jean Labadie looked at them closely, thinking that they looked mighty like the feathers his own chickens had worn before they'd disappeared. Still and all, you couldn't tell a man, 'These look like my chickens' feathers.' So Jean Labadie didn't say anything about them. He just kept cutting brush and thinking.

'If André thought I had a dog,' Jean Labadie said to himself, 'maybe he'd keep away from my chicken yard.' So right then and there, Jean Labadie made up a big lie. He invented a dog. He said to André, 'Have you seen my big black dog yet?'

'Dog?' André said. 'You don't have any dog.'

'I didn't use to have a dog,' Jean Labadie said, 'but now I do. I just bought him from the Indians. Somebody's been stealing my chickens, so I went out and got myself a dog. He's big and black and mighty mean, and I don't think anyone will do any more prowling around my chicken yard.'

'Well, well, so you've got a dog now,' André remarked.

Jean Labadie looked up.

'See, there he goes now, black as coal, with his big red tongue hanging out.'

André looked.

'I don't see any dog,' he said.

'What do you mean, you don't see any dog?' Jean Labadie said. 'There he goes, right across that ridge.'

'Where?' André asked.

'Look, man, look. Don't you see him lifting those big black paws one after another?'

'Yes, yes, I see him now!' André said, straining his eyes for a sight of the big dog with the hanging red tongue and the paws going one after another. 'Yes, he looks mighty mean, slinking along the fence like that.'

Jean Labadie said nothing more about the dog he had just invented. André Drouillard was a little quiet about it all, but once in a while he looked up towards the ridge to catch a glimpse of the animal.

Jean was right about one thing. There were no more chickens stolen from his chicken yard. He was pretty pleased with himself.

Then one day he met André on the road.

'I saw your big black dog today,' André said. 'He was running along the fence, his red tongue hanging out, and his big feet going one after another. I got out of his way pretty fast, you can bet your life.'

Jean Labadie was amused, but he was also a little disgusted with André's imagination. If the big black dog was running around the countryside, who was guarding the chicken yard?

André met Jean Labadie again on the road one day and said, 'Jean, I saw your big black dog this morning. He was on the other side of town chasing rabbits.'

Jean said, 'Must be some other dog, André. My big black dog is at home guarding the chicken yard.'

'If it wasn't your big black dog whose was it?' André said. 'Doesn't your dog have a big red tongue that hangs out? When he runs, doesn't he fan the air with his feet?'

'Well, it sounds like my dog,' Jean said, 'but just the same he's at home now watching the chicken yard.'

'You'd better chain him up,' André said. 'People in town are complaining about your letting a wild Indian dog like that run loose.'

Jean wanted to ask how people found out about his dog, but he decided to keep quiet. If he had a dog, people obviously had to know about it.

A few days later André stopped Jean Labadie again. This time he spoke sharply. 'You're going to have to do something about that vicious dog of yours. Today on the road he came at me and snapped at my legs. I had to beat him off with a stick.'

Jean Labadie didn't know whether to laugh or call André Drouillard a liar. The big black dog had gotten pretty real by now. Finally he said, 'All right, I guess I'll have to chain him up.' He put his fingers in his mouth and gave a loud whistle. 'Here, boy! Here, boy!' he called to the dog. André Drouillard looked around nervously and left in a hurry.

For a while Jean Labadie heard no more about it. Then one day when he was in the store buying roofing nails, Madame Villeneuve came up to him and said, 'Jean Labadie, you ought to be ashamed the way you let that fierce dog run loose in town.'

'He's a fierce dog, that's true,' Jean Labadie replied, 'but he's chained up at home.'

'Maybe he *was* chained up,' Madame Villeneuve said, 'but he's not chained up any more. He's running around with his red tongue hanging out, making his big black paws go this way and that way. He even bared his teeth at me this afternoon.'

Jean Labadie began to worry. It looked like things were getting out of control with the dog. He thought maybe he ought to get rid of him. So he said to Madame Villeneuve, 'I'll tell you what I'll do, Madame Villeneuve. Tomorrow morning I'll take that dog back to the Indians.'

'It's about time,' Madame Villeneuve said.

The next morning Jean hitched his horse and got in the cart. He waited until he saw André Drouillard, then he whistled loudly and made a great show of getting the dog in with him. As he drove past André's house, André shouted, 'Taking him back, Jean?'

'Back where I got him,' Jean Labadie replied, and he drove down the road and headed for the Indian village.

He spent the day talking with his Indian friends, and in the late afternoon he headed for home. As he came around the bend near André Drouillard's house, a feeling of foreboding came over him. He saw André waiting at the gate.

'What's the matter?' Jean Labadie asked.

'Plenty's the matter,' André said. 'Your big black dog's come home. Beat you here by an hour. I was just coming out to milk, and what should I see but the dog coming up the road, his big red tongue hanging out of his mouth.'

Jean Labadie exploded. 'André Drouillard,' he shouted, 'you're a liar! I just left that big black dog with the Indians!'

'Oh?' André said coldly. 'Now you're calling your neighbours liars?' And he turned and went into the house.

Jean Labadie groaned. After all the pains he'd gone to, he had messed everything up. Now he had called André Drouillard a liar. He might as well have called him a chicken thief in the first place.

The way it turned out, Madame Villeneuve saw the big black dog running behind her house. Henri Dupuis saw him skulking behind the store. Delphine Langlois saw him running through the graveyard. And everyone was angry at Jean Labadie. But Jean figured there was no use taking the dog to the Indian village again, he'd just come back.

A few days later, when Jean Labadie was sitting in front of the blacksmith's shop, André Drouillard came riding up at a great pace on his horse. 'Where is Dr Brisson?' André shouted. 'Somebody get Dr Brisson!'

'What's the matter?' everyone called out at once.

André raised a bleeding hand and pointed it at Jean Labadie.

'*His* big black dog bit me!' he said.

Jean sat there with his mouth open. Seeing a dog that isn't there is one thing. Being bitten by such a dog is something else again. He closed his mouth and went over where everyone was looking at André's bleeding hand.

'It doesn't look like a dog bite to me, it looks more like an axe cut,' Jean Labadie said.

This made everyone angry. 'First he lets his wild Indian dog run loose,' they said, 'and then when someone gets bitten he says it's an axe cut!'

Jean felt very helpless about the dog. At last he said, 'My friends, I think we'll have to put an end to this matter once and for all. I'll give André two chickens for the damage to his hand. And what's more important, I think I'll have to shoot that big black dog.'

The crowd was silent. Jean Labadie said, 'Follow me.' He walked down the road to his house, with the crowd behind. He went in the door and came out a minute later with his gun. 'Stand here,' Jean Labadie said, 'and watch me kill the big black dog.'

He went out by the barn and whistled. He whistled again. Then he called out, 'Here he comes!'

The crowd moved back toward the fence to get out of the way. Madame Villeneuve said tensely, 'I see him behind the barn, with his big red tongue hanging out!' And André Drouillard said, 'Also with his big old feet going up and down!'

Jean Labadie raised his gun to his shoulder, aimed carefully, and fired. 'Got him,' he said. Delphine Langlois fainted.

'There,' Jean Labadie said softly, brushing a tear from his eye, 'I've done it. My big black dog is gone for good.'

Everyone agreed that Jean Labadie's dog was done for, and they turned and went away. André Drouillard headed for home with two fat chickens under his arm.

As for Jean Labadie, when the people looked over their shoulders they saw him sadly digging a grave for the only dog he ever had.

Acknowledgements

Roger D. Abrahams: 'Hankering for a Long Tail' from *Afro-American Folktales*, edited by Roger D. Abrahams, Copyright © 1985 by Roger D. Abrahams, reprinted by permission of Pantheon Books, a division of Random House, Inc. **Richard Chase:** 'The Two Old Women's Bet' from *The Grandfather Tales*, Copyright © 1948, renewed 1976 by Richard Chase, reprinted by permission of the publisher, Houghton Mifflin Co. All rights reserved. **Padraic Colum:** 'The Boy Pu Nia and the King of the Sharks' from *Legends of Hawaii* (1937), reprinted by permission of the publisher, Yale University Press. **Harold Courlander:** 'The Coming of Asin' and 'Jean Labadie's Dog' both from Harold Courlander (ed.): *Ride with the Sun* (McGraw Hill, for the United Nations Women's Guild, 1955); 'The Tiger's Whisker' from *The Tiger's Whisker and Other Tales and Legends from Asia and the Pacific* (Methuen, 1960), copyright holder not traced. **Kevin Crossley-Holland:** 'To Tell the Truth', Copyright © Kevin Crossley-Holland 1998, first published in *The Young Oxford Book of Folk Tales* (OUP, 1998), reproduced by permission of the author c/o Rogers, Coleridge & White Ltd, 20 Powis Mews, London W11 1JN. **Mercedes Dorson** and **Jeanne Wilmot:** 'The Legend of the Yara' from *Tales from the Rain Forest*, Copyright © 1997 by Mercedes Dorson and Jeanne Wilmot, reprinted by permission of HarperCollins Publishers Inc. **Richard Erdoes** and **Alfonzo Ortiz:** 'The Spirit-Wife' from *American Indian Myths and Legends*, Copyright © 1984 by Richard Erdoes and Alfonzo Ortiz, reprinted by permission of Pantheon Books, a division of Random House, Inc. **Helen** and **William McAlpine**: 'The Tongue-Cut Sparrow' from *Japanese Tales and Legends* (OUP, 1958), reprinted by permission of Mrs Lily L. Gillespie and Mrs Mary Johnson, executors of the Estate of the authors, c/o Millar, Shearer and Black, Cookstown, Northern Ireland. **Eric Maddern:** 'The Rainbow Bird and the Crocodile and How the People First Got Fire', retelling of an aboriginal tale, used by permission of the author. **Eric** and **Nancy Protter:** 'The Magic Brocade' from *Folk and Fairy Tales of Far-Off Lands* (Duell, Sloan & Pearce, 1965), Copyright 1965 by Eric and Nancy Protter, reprinted by permission of Eric Protter. **A. K. Ramanujan:** 'Why the Fish Laughed' from *Folktales from India*, Copyright © 1991 by A. K. Ramanujan, reprinted by permission of Pantheon Books, a division of Random House, Inc. **Philip Sherlock:** 'Tiger Story, Anansi Story' from *West Indian Folk-tales* (OUP, 1966), copyright holder not traced. **Frances Toor:** 'The Hungry Peasant, God, and Death' from *A Treasury of Mexican Folkways*, Copyright © 1947, 1975 by Crown

Publishers, Inc., reprinted by permission of Crown Publishers, a division of Random House, Inc. **Irina Zheleznova:** 'Kotura, Lord of the Winds' from *Folk Tales from Russian Lands* (Dover, 1969), by permission of Dover Publications, Inc.

Although we have tried to trace and contact all copyright holders before publication this has not been possible in every case. If notified we will rectify any errors or omissions at the earliest opportunity.

We also acknowledge with thanks the following out-of-copyright material: **Joseph Jacobs:** 'The Son of Seven Queens' from *Indian Fairy Tales*. **Andrew Lang:** 'The Bones of Djulung' from *The Lilac Fairy Book*.

The editor is grateful to Margaret Lockerbie Cameron, Keith Harrison, Ron Heapy, David Lumsdaine, Eric Maddern, Linda Waslien, and Gillian Crossley-Holland for their valuable advice and pursuit of elusive tales.